HIDDEN WITCH

TORRENT WITCHES COZY MYSTERIES
BOOK THREE

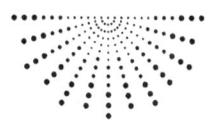

TESS LAKE

TESS LAKE

ALSO BY TESS LAKE

Torrent Witches Cozy Mysteries

Butter Witch (Torrent Witches Cozy Mysteries #1)

Treasure Witch (Torrent Witches Cozy Mysteries #2)

Hidden Witch (Torrent Witches Cozy Mysteries #3)

Fabulous Witch (Torrent Witches Cozy Mysteries #4)

Holiday Witch (Torrent Witches Cozy Mysteries #5)

Shadow Witch (Torrent Witches Cozy Mysteries #6)

Love Witch (Torrent Witches Cozy Mysteries #7)

Cozy Witch (Torrent Witches Cozy Mysteries #8)

Lost Witch (Torrent Witches Cozy Mysteries #9)

Wicked Witch (Torrent Witches Cozy Mysteries #10)

Box Sets

Torrent Witches Box Set #1 (Butter Witch, Treasure Witch, Hidden Witch)

Torrent Witches Box Set #2 (Fabulous Witch, Holiday Witch, Shadow Witch)

Audiobooks

Butter Witch

Treasure Witch

Hidden Witch

Torrent Witches Box Set #1 (Butter Witch, Treasure Witch, Hidden Witch)

Fabulous Witch

Holiday Witch

Shadow Witch

Torrent Witches Box Set #2 (Fabulous Witch, Holiday Witch, Shadow Witch)

Love Witch

Cozy Witch

Lost Witch

Wicked Witch

Hidden Witch Copyright © 2016 Tess Lake. ALL RIGHTS RESERVED. This book contains material protected under International and Federal Copyright Laws and Treaties. Any unauthorized reprint or use of this material is prohibited. No part of this book may be reproduced or transmitted in any form or by any means, electronic or mechanical, including photocopying, recording, or by any information storage and retrieval system without express written permission from the author.
Tess Lake

Tesslake.com

This is a work of fiction. The characters, incidents and dialogs in this book are of the author's imagination and are not to be construed as real. Any resemblance to actual events or persons, living or dead, is completely coincidental.

CHAPTER ONE

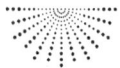

The house was fully ablaze by the time I got there. The third fire in as many weeks. The first one (in an empty warehouse) was written off as just one of those things that happens. An accident. The second was an empty vacation home that burned to the ground. It was about then people started whispering *arson.*

Now with the third, they'd be yelling it.

The house was one of a row all built in the 1950s. They had spectacular sea views and were built of very flammable timber from top to bottom in that very special time when building codes weren't really adhered to very well.

To sum it up: they may as well have built these houses out of literal matches that had been soaked in gasoline.

I had my camera in my hands but I just couldn't bring myself to take a photo. One of the neighbors was shouting there was still someone inside.

The firefighters were doing their best to contain the blaze. There were two fire engines, and the men were pouring hundreds of gallons of water in through the broken windows, but it didn't seem to be having any effect. Sheriff

Hardy was on the scene yelling at onlookers to get back. It seemed the entire street had come out to watch. I saw Carter Wilkins on the far side of the street taking photos left-handed. His right arm was in a sling for some reason. Whatever it was, I didn't know and I didn't care. I'd had just about enough of him and his eyebrows for a lifetime.

I'd been at home lazing around when I'd seen the curls of smoke rising up above Harlot Bay. I'd immediately raced (as fast as you can "race" in a very old car) into town, a fire engine screaming by me on the way.

"She's still in there!" one of the neighbors yelled out.

The firemen put on breathing gear, heavy masks and gloves. They smashed the front door open and rushed into the cloud of smoke. It must've only been a minute, but it felt like ages before they came running back out through the front door carrying an unconscious elderly woman between them. They moved around behind the fire engine and immediately put an oxygen mask on her face. It was a minute more before the ambulance arrived and the paramedics took over, loading her into the back of the ambulance before slamming the door shut and racing off to the hospital.

The firefighters continued to pour water on the blaze and it wasn't long before the flames finally gave up. The smoke changed color to thick black and the red flames ceased flickering in the windows.

I was standing there watching the firefighters pour water into the smoking house when I felt that intuition tingle on the back of my neck. I turned around, expecting to see someone watching me, but there wasn't anyone there. There was a crowd of police officers and locals, but whoever it was that had been watching me had shifted their gaze.

I took the time to look over the crowd. They say arsonists will often return to the scene of the crime. This part of Harlot Bay was mostly older people, so most of the crowd was at least sixty and over, retired or very close to it. I was pretty sure the old guy wearing board shorts and a Hawaiian shirt wasn't the suspect.

I finally managed to get myself to take a few photos of the smoking house, my ancient camera taking about a minute between photos. I didn't really want to report on arson, and given the *Harlot Bay Reader* was virtually failing on all cylinders, it was becoming clear I wasn't *really* a reporter but just someone running a blog that was never going to go anywhere.

Sheriff Hardy was busy talking to someone, so I decided to go home.

My car took three tries to get going, and on the way back to Torrent Mansion it made some horrible squealing noises that sounded very expensive. Now that Molly and Luce were making a bit of money with their coffee shop, they'd offered to lend me some money to get my car repaired, but I just couldn't say yes. I had to make a go of things myself. As much as I appreciated the offer of charity, I couldn't accept it.

I got back to our end of the mansion, where only Adams awaited me, sleeping on the sofa. Molly and Luce were with their respective boyfriends, Ollie and Will. The moms were away at some sort of business convention for the weekend, and they'd taken Aunt Cass with them. Apart from Grandma, frozen down in the basement and staring at nothing, I was by myself.

I put my camera down on the table and went to make myself hot coffee (despite it being the end of summer and the temperature sitting at "melt ice cream" level). I'd gotten into the habit of frequently making myself drinks and little snacks so I could avoid having a moment to think about things.

Things mostly being Jack Bishop.

It had been the start of summer when he'd returned to

Canada to settle his business, and although he'd said it would only be a few weeks, it was nearly the end of summer now, and he still wasn't back.

True to his word, he'd written me letters. In the first, he'd pretended he was on an Antarctic expedition in the eighteen hundreds. He had written about the cold and the penguins and filled the letter with jokes and happy things. I had written back to him, pretending I was on an expedition through the Siberian wilderness. And that's how it had gone for roughly eleven weeks, both of us pretending to be people other than who we were.

I was looking forward to Jack returning, but somewhere inside me there was a deep ache. It came from a spike of fear I could not remove. I was pretending in letters and pretending in real life too. I'm a witch, but I was pretending I was not.

I finished making my coffee and tried to shake those thoughts out of my head. They say absence makes the heart grow fonder, but they forget to add it also makes the mind go crazy and the nights grow sleepless. They forget to say absence pulls on your heart until something snaps because you can't feel that kind of pain any longer without going crazy. And so you stop caring just because you can't bear it any longer.

Wow! Sorry, I'm getting really dark and morbid here. I think it's because I'm living in the middle of the romance capital at the moment. Molly and Ollie, Goddess bless their cotton socks, are disgustingly cute. Luce and Will even more so. My cousins are enjoying life, love and their boyfriends.

And... I get to sleep in the next room.

I think they expected that when Jack returns, we'd instantly be boyfriend and girlfriend and on the same level as they were. The truth is, we'd hardly gone out on any dates, and although we were writing letters, we didn't really know each other at all.

I turned on the television and finally managed to get my thoughts out of the dark patch where they'd strayed. That's how I spent the end of the afternoon: watching mindless television and, after Adams woke up, talking to him. The local news reported on the fire in a thirty-second bit, adding at the end, "It is the third fire in as many weeks."

All journalists write the same way.

I was pondering dinner and another early night when I got a phone call from a blocked number.

"Hello?"

"Harlow, it's Sheriff Hardy."

"Hi, Sheriff… what can I do for you?" I said, a little uncertain. I had his number stored, so I don't know why it came up as blocked.

"I have some information I need you to keep private. I'm trusting you a lot with this."

He paused for a moment and then sighed. I felt a flutter of anxiety in my stomach. What was going on?

"Well, you were at the fire today, so you probably know we've had three fires in the last three weeks. I got word from an old friend of mine that a special arson investigator is going to be coming to Harlot Bay. He's going to be investigating you."

"Me?" I managed to get out.

"Apparently he knows the old apartment building burnt down, and then there was a fire up at the mansion. I'm not sure how much else he knows, but it's a matter of record that Zero Bend's house burned down after you were there as well. You never made it into any reports about the lighthouse fire, but I would definitely be on your guard. I have to tell you something else too – you can't call me anymore and you can't come to the police station. This guy is going to be going through phone records, and from what I hear he's a real head kicker. I don't want him to find anything suspicious in those records."

That tiny flicker of anxiety in my stomach was now a ball of ice. The fact is, Sheriff Hardy knew on some level there was something strange going on with the Torrents. I wasn't entirely sure *what he knew*, but he had certainly called on us in the past and we'd delivered. I knew vaguely that Aunt Cass had done some work with the police department as well, unofficially. Sheriff Hardy had shared plenty of information with me under the guise of me being a journalist, when really he was just trying to solve crimes.

"Does this mean I'm a suspect or something? Should I get a lawyer?"

"I think it would be best you consider getting legal advice if this guy comes asking questions. His name is Detective James Moreland. We both know you had nothing to do with the fire at the apartment or at your property or at Zero Bend's. I know you don't have anything to do with the fires in Harlot Bay over the last three weeks, or any of the other ones that haven't made the news. But cases have been made on circumstantial evidence, so you and your family need to be very careful."

I was still sitting on the sofa, but it felt like the whole room was whirling. What Sheriff Hardy didn't know was that the night the apartment had burnt down was the same night my loser ex-boyfriend had dumped me because I'd lost my job. I'd gone to sleep with Adams by my side and awoken to the sound of fire sirens. The entire apartment complex had burnt down, and although they'd blamed faulty wiring in the end, I knew the truth. I'd Slipped.

When I'd returned home with nothing more than my cat, my car, my laptop and the clothes on my back, the magic inside me had lashed out just a few days later, burning down the house on the property where my family had been living.

As a result of that, the moms had gone into deep debt to renovate the center of the Torrent Mansion and what we call the East Wing, where Molly, Luce and I live.

That was all over a year ago now, and although I was certain I hadn't started any more fires in my sleep, there was certainly a lot of circumstantial evidence connecting me in any case.

"Okay, well... thanks for telling me, Sheriff. I really appreciate it."

"It'll be okay, Harlow. He's only here to look at the arson, and as soon as we figure out whether it is just a bad run of coincidence or someone actually setting fires, then he'll leave."

"Do you think it really could be arson? The first place was just a warehouse and the second was an empty vacation home. It seems random."

"I really don't know. Harlot Bay seems to go through a bad batch of fires every few decades or so, and with all the dodgy houses and bad wiring, it's hard to know really whether there's someone behind it."

Sheriff Hardy sounded exhausted when he said that. Like he'd had a very long day.

"What happened to the woman they took out of the house?" I asked.

Another sigh from Sheriff Hardy.

"Her name was Lenora Gray. She was eighty-one years old and she died of smoke inhalation about an hour ago."

"That's terrible," I whispered.

"It's murder if someone is behind it. Okay, I need to go now. If I talk to you again, it's only going to be in an official capacity until the investigator is gone."

"Thanks, Sheriff," I said and then he hung up.

I sat on the sofa for a while staring into nothing, wishing someone would come home so I could talk to them. Adams is great, but he's a cat and most of his solutions to problems involve eating something.

Honestly, *not such a bad idea.*

Molly and Luce would be back tomorrow and we had a game of Scrabble planned, along with some drinks. As that thought entered my mind, I remembered there was still a bottle of red wine in the fridge. I poured myself a glass and then downed it in one gulp. Lenora Gray was her name and she'd died in a fire. A deep sadness washed over me and a tear trickled down my cheek.

CHAPTER TWO

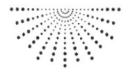

"Jarqel? What does that mean exactly?" Luce asked, crossing her arms.

Molly topped off our glasses of red wine before answering.

"Jarqel? Oh, I'm surprised you don't know it. It's a cooking term. It means to microwave something, usually meat, waaaaay too high and then fry it in a desperate attempt to make it not disgusting. You know, like how you cook most of the time."

"I do not jarqel my food! I didn't notice the microwave was set on high is all!" Luce said indignantly.

I counted up the points.

"Twenty-two!"

"Yes!" Molly gave a fist pump and we clinked our glasses together in celebration.

"I'll jarqel you," Luce muttered.

I'd woken with a slight headache, courtesy of the possibly one too many glasses of wine I'd had last night. The night of sleep had helped improve my mood. Yes, Sheriff Hardy was unable to talk to me and, yes, there was possibly some kind of special investigator coming to throw me in jail, but it was Sunday, I was with my cousins, and while it's true you can't buy happiness, you can certainly buy board games and wine and that's pretty much the same thing.

The day was warm and it stretched out ahead of us, filled with red wine, good food and our house rules version of Scrabble. If you could explain a word convincingly, it was allowed.

Hence Luce playing "MTREASURE" next.

"Explain," I said, sipping my wine.

"MTreasure is a shortened form of MaybeTreasure, as in when you find hidden treasure but then it's taken away from you and you might get it back but probably not."

"Topical," Molly commented.

"Is a single gold coin really treasure, do you think?" I asked.

About a week after competing in the Gold Mud Run, we'd taken our shovels and gone to the hidden cave where I'd seen ghostly pirates murdering each other over a chest of treasure. I'd promised one pirate in particular that we'd lay his bones to rest. It wasn't all altruistic, though – they had buried a chest filled to the brim with treasure.

We'd dug down and found bones. No treasure chest. No millions in gold coins. After removing all the bones, we found a single solitary coin, which then prompted the great "keep it or hand it in" debate.

Aunt Cass was very firmly on the Keep It side of things. My mother was not.

We'd reburied the bones in a nearby field and held a small ceremony to lay them to rest. No ghosts had appeared, but we could all feel the change in the magic after we were done. Then we'd carried on our argument all the way to the ferry, back to the mainland and to the house.

Mom finally won by snatching up the coin and disappearing with it into town. She handed it in, giving a false location where she found it, and now the coin was stuck in a limbo of Finders Keepers vs. Important Historical Treasure.

Essentially, Luce was right: it was MTreasure, and it was a very big *maybe* that we'd end up with it.

"It was a solid gold coin. I think that counts as treasure," Luce said.

"It's an abbreviation!" Molly complained.

"I'll allow it," I said. I sipped my wine and sighed in pleasure.

That moment of contemplating peaceful happiness lasted approximately four point five seconds, until an all-black car drove up to the mansion and squealed to a stop outside. The man who got out was tall and thin and wearing what could only be described as "Some Kind of Law Enforcement Outfit, Standard Issue #5." Think white shirt, black pants, shiny shoes and that indefinable air that suggests you've done something wrong and it's only a matter of time until they find out what it is.

My warm red wine buzz swooshed out of me, leaving behind crackling adrenaline. Something was about to go very wrong. Was this the investigator?

We went to the front door and opened it before the man could knock. He looked at me and then over my shoulders at Luce and Molly, who'd followed with full glasses of wine in their hands.

"Having a party, I see."

Not a question. His voice was light but he wasn't friendly.

"Red wine and Scrabble!" Luce called out from behind me.

The man nodded and pulled out a notepad. He wrote something down. Surely not *red wine and Scrabble?*

"Ms. Torrent, you're a hard woman to get in contact with. Did you get any of my calls?"

My hand strayed to my phone in my pocket. It has been dropped a million times but it still worked most of the time. The magical energy in Harlot Bay isn't kind to modern telecommunications. I couldn't tell him this, so I shook my head instead.

The man flashed a badge in front of me.

"I'm Special Investigator Detective James Moreland. I'm here about the fire that destroyed an apartment building known as The Meadows. I believe you were one of the people living there at the time. May we speak?"

My answer died in my throat and I let out something that sounded like *gurk*.

Special Investigator? Oh crap.

CHAPTER THREE

I was standing there with my mouth open like a fish when Aunt Cass appeared out of nowhere and sauntered up to the front door.

"Thought I could smell bacon," she said, looking Detective Moreland up and down.

"I'm here to interview Harlow," he said.

"No, you're not. Harlow isn't available for an interview. If you wish to question her about anything, then you need to arrest her. Now go away."

Aunt Cass didn't wait for a response. She slammed the door in his face.

I suspect Detective Moreland was a seasoned professional and used to having doors slammed in his face. He didn't yell out (which is what I would've done). He simply returned to his car and drove away.

"Go Aunt Cass," Molly commented. Aunt Cass whirled around, but then saw Molly was not being sarcastic (for a change).

"Well, if the Internet has taught us anything, it's that you don't talk to police."

"Why is he after Harlow, though?" Luce asked worriedly.

"She was at the scene of a few fires, so they're going to try to pin it on her nice and easy. They won't succeed, though," Aunt Cass said, looking at me meaningfully.

Near the start of the summer, Aunt Cass's cottage full of fireworks had exploded one night. We'd tried to cover it up as a special event we were putting on for the guests of the Torrent Mansion Bed-and-Breakfast.

After the fire, I'd detected a magical scent. It appeared the fire had been started by a witch or some other magical entity.

Aunt Cass didn't talk much about it, but I had the distinct impression she was still investigating who'd blown up her stash of illegal fireworks.

I suddenly realized Aunt Cass wasn't supposed to be here.

"Weren't you away with the moms?" I said.

"That business convention was boring. I came back."

"How? Did you drive here?" I asked.

"Yes, darling, that's right. I, a powerful Slip Witch, hopped in my invisible car and drove back here. Use your brain, please."

Well, there went that moment of happy family bonding. Before we could break out into a bout of snarking at each other, though, another shiny black car pulled up out the front of the house.

It was Dominic Gresso, real estate agent and developer. A long while ago I had written an article about him after his business partner had tried to embezzle funds and then pin it on Dominic. After the investigation, Dominic had come out clean and his business partner had gone to jail after being virtually run out of town. I know this makes it sound like Dominic is actually the good guy and his business partner was the bad guy, but the truth is they're more like two sleazy bad guys in business together and one did some bad things he got caught for. Dominic is in his forties, has a head of magnificent thick black hair and is quite overweight, though he wears tailored suits to hide it.

He knocked on the front door with his pudgy hand. Aunt Cass opened it and he looked at us in surprise. I'm not sure he was expecting to find Aunt Cass and the three of us standing behind the door, holding glasses of red wine.

"Yes, what is it, Gresso?" Aunt Cass said.

She seemed to be in a particularly spiky mood today, and I reminded myself not to get on her bad side.

"Good afternoon, Cassandra. I was wondering if April was available?"

Molly, Luce and I resisted sharing a glance, although I could feel we were about to. Our grandma, April Torrent, is frozen in the basement and has been for at least twenty years. The short explanation is: something magical went wrong.

"She's not available. What is it you want?" Aunt Cass said.

Dominic took a shiny white card business card out of his pocket and tried to pass it to Aunt Cass, who just stared at it like he was trying to hand her a piece of poo. After a moment of awkwardness, he handed the card to Molly, who took it reluctantly.

"Well, I've seen what you've all been doing with the mansion up here and I think it's amazing. I want to talk about buying the property and developing it. I think we would be looking at well over a million if you're interested in selling. Would it be possible for April to give me a call as soon as she is available?"

"We're not selling," Aunt Cass said, flatly.

"I understand it can be an emotional topic. I really do have a good offer for you. We can preserve the mansion if that's what you're concerned about."

"What I am concerned about, Gresso, is that when you were twelve years old you came to my front door telling me you were selling cookies for charity. I put in an order for a box of mint chocolate chip cookies and then I never saw you again. What happened to my order?" Aunt Cass said, sarcasm dripping off every word.

Dominic flushed red and looked down at the ground, for a minute I think reverting back to that twelve-year-old boy who had probably been running some sort of scam to make money off people in the neighborhood. Then he cleared his throat and got himself back together.

"I have no idea what you're talking about. It must have been someone else."

"I want my box of mint chocolate chip cookies. Until it is delivered, there's not going to be any discussion with anybody," Aunt Cass said.

I'm sure Dominic had planned to come up here and stay calm and happy the whole time. He just hadn't counted on Aunt Cass, who can rub anyone the wrong way, including a real estate agent dedicated to keeping that fake smile plastered on.

"As I understand it, April Torrent is the legal owner of this land, and as I further understand it, no one has seen her for a number of years. Perhaps she moved away? I've been trying to get in contact with her and I can't find any other addresses for her other than this one. You know, the funny thing is it looks like she just vanished. My investigators can't find a trace of her. Could you imagine that? She vanishes and her family pretends she's still around? So how about you get her to give me a call when she's available."

Dominic marched his way back to the car, leaving us standing there speechless. It was only once he was driving away that Aunt Cass slammed the door shut.

"Oh Goddess, is he threatening us?" Luce said.

"It sounded like a threat to me," I said.

"He's not gonna do anything," Aunt Cass said. Even

though she said it with her usual bluster, I could see she was shaken. She certainly hadn't expected he would come back at her so hard.

"It's easy – one of us calls him and pretends to be Grandma. Say we don't want to sell and that's it," Molly said.

"Forget it, it's fine. Now put down the glasses of wine and come with me back to the so-called East Wing."

I think we were all in a state of shock: first at the investigator turning up, and then at the confrontation between Dominic and Aunt Cass. So that's why we followed her directions to hurry up clearing out the spare room pronto.

"What do we have to empty this for?" Molly asked, waving her arm at the assorted boxes and random bits of junk that had collected at the end of the bed.

We heard a car pull up outside our end of the mansion.

"Someone staying here. She's here now," Aunt Cass said, looking out the window.

We followed Aunt Cass to the front door to find Hattie Stern dropping off a sullen teenage girl. I didn't know her name, but I knew she was Hattie Stern's granddaughter. I'd only seen her once, sometime ago at Hattie's when I'd gone there for training (which was now finished, hooray!).

She got out of the car and shuffled her way around to the trunk, where she pulled out a bag. Hattie was staring straight ahead. As soon as the girl closed the trunk, Hattie nodded to Aunt Cass, who, incredibly, nodded back. Then Hattie drove away, leaving us with the teenage girl standing in front of our house. Aunt Cass immediately took charge.

"Okay, now that the old biddy is gone, let's get moving. I'm Cass, that's Harlow, Luce and Molly. Everyone, this is Kira Stern. She is a Slip Witch and will be staying here for a while to train with me. Okay?"

"Hi," Luce said.

"Nice to meet you," Molly said.

Kira was maybe sixteen or seventeen. The last time I'd seen her, she'd had purple dye in her hair. Now it was blond with a pink streak in it. She had a silver nose ring as well.

She looked so young and fragile that for a moment I wanted to rush over and give her a hug. Then, like all teenagers, she opened her mouth.

"Great, get to stay with some old people. *Love* being dumped off."

"Old people?" Molly muttered.

"Welcome to our home!" Luce said, walking over to her.

Kira did the typical looking-up-and-down-with-disdain teenager thing.

It was Aunt Cass who came to the rescue.

"Put your bag inside, and then you and Harlow come with me to the main house," she instructed.

Kira turned her disdain towards Aunt Cass, but then quickly looked away. She had enough sense to know not to tangle with her.

Kira followed us inside. We did a very quick ten-second clean of the bedroom that she'd be staying in, hauling boxes out and dumping them in the common area. She threw her bag on the bed and then followed us back out to the kitchen.

"So you guys, like, *live* here?" she asked, looking around. That teenage disdain was back.

"Yeah, we do and it's awesome," Molly said a little snarkily.

Before that could develop any further, Ollie and Will pulled up at the front door in Ollie's car. There were five seconds of introductions where Ollie and Will both said hello to Kira and she shyly smiled back at them. Then they were gone, leaving me and Kira alone. She turned to me.

"So where's *your* boyfriend?" she asked.

Was I this annoying as a teenager? I don't remember

being a judgmental little snark, but who knows? Maybe I was.

"I don't have a boyfriend."

"*Right...*" Kira said, drawing the word out.

"Do you remember me? I saw you at your grandmother's house. I was training with her."

"Nope."

Kira's phone buzzed in her pocket and she had it out in a flash, tapping away and ignoring me.

"Okay, well, come with me down to the main house and we'll see what Aunt Cass wants."

Kira ignored me, continuing to tap on her phone.

Fine, two could play that game. I walked out of the house and made my way down to the main part of the mansion. When I was about halfway there, I heard Kira come out and rush after me. When she finally caught up, I didn't say anything.

"I was coming, I had to talk to someone," she muttered.

We went in through the dining room to find Aunt Cass sitting in front of the television, watching yet another police detective show. She flicked it off as soon as we arrived and stood up.

"The two of you are not going to talk about what you're about to see today, okay?" Aunt Cass said, pointing a finger at both of us.

"Um... okay?" Kira said.

"Enough with the dramatics," I said.

"Snitches end up in ditches," Aunt Cass said, wiggling her finger at me. "This way."

We followed her back through the kitchen and down the stairs into the basement. Grandma, as usual, was standing in the back corner, still frozen in time with her hands out in front of her. She had a concealment spell on her, which excluded family members. Aunt Cass waved a hand and Kira gasped as Grandma appeared.

"Oh my Goddess," she said.

"Tell anyone and I'll curse you back to the Stone Age," Aunt Cass said. She grabbed the flashlight by the door that led to the underfloor of the house.

"What happened to her?"

"She attempted some dangerous magic," Aunt Cass said.

Unbelievable. She won't tell *us* a thing, but the moment someone from outside the family shows up, she spills that Grandma attempted some dangerous magic?

Aunt Cass flicked on the flashlight and opened the old door, and we followed her in.

"Be careful where you walk. Some of the floorboards are rotting and there's another entire story below us," I told Kira.

She didn't say anything but did turn on her phone light.

At first I thought we were heading for Aunt Cass's underground laboratory, but then we took a right instead of a left and headed down a corridor I was sure I'd never seen before. It ended in a heavy door. Aunt Cass grunted when she opened it.

We followed her into a room that looked like something out of a serial killer's fantasy.

You know in those cop shows how there is always a moment when they have the big map covered with strings and pins and there are photographs stuck to the wall and random newspaper articles all over the place? Aunt Cass done *that* to this room. One entire wall was a gigantic map of Harlot Bay and its surrounds. I counted at least eight different pin colors. Tangled around the pins were bits of crisscrossed thread with no apparent pattern. The map had question marks and notes written all over it.

I walked over to the map to take a closer look and then felt a push of magic from behind me. Between one blink and the next, most of the pins on the map vanished, leaving only a few red ones behind.

She'd seriously cast a concealment spell to stop *me* from looking at the map?

"What did you do that for?" I asked, turning around. I saw the rest of the walls were blank now too.

"I need you to help me with this, and all the rest of that stuff would just confuse you," Aunt Cass said, fixing me with a challenging look.

Or you just like showing off, I thought.

"You need us to help you?" Kira asked.

"Around the beginning of the summer, something set off a magical fire in my stash of fireworks up in one of the cottages behind the mansion. They destroyed many hundreds of dollars' worth of stock and cost me possibly thousands of dollars' worth of profit. I have been investigating this for some months and have come to the conclusion it appears to be a magical entity of some type. Given the recent fires in Harlot Bay, I believe we are dealing with a fire spirit of some kind, and I need your help, both of you, to track it down."

"A fire spirit? So all the red pins are recent fires?" I asked.

"All reported and unreported fires I've been able to discover. Whatever it is keeps moving around, so what I need you to do is take the three beacons over there and place them in three specific locations so we can triangulate a position for whatever this thing is. Understand?"

The beacons were essentially pieces of carved crystal, with a raven's feather and some other bits and pieces, bound up with string.

"You think the fire yesterday out on the coast was caused by a fire spirit?" I asked.

"*Duh*, that's what she just said," Kira said to me.

"I like her. She gets it," Aunt Cass said. She picked up the beacons and handed them to Kira while I tried not to glare.

"You'll be in charge of these. Here are the addresses of the places where I need you to put them up. Now get going. I need it done right now."

Aunt Cass waved the list of addresses at me.

"Wait, I want more information. If there is a fire spirit somewhere in Harlot Bay, what are you going to do with it when you find it?"

Aunt Cass shrugged.

"I'm not sure yet. Maybe trap it and deport it. Or if it won't cooperate, I might have to extinguish it."

"Let's do it. I'm ready," Kira said.

Teenagers. So easily swayed and so desperate for approval.

"Okay, give me the addresses," I muttered.

CHAPTER FOUR

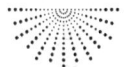

The first location on Aunt Cass's list was the old lighthouse. It was on the far side of Harlot Bay, out on the bluffs overlooking the ocean.

I drove down the hill, heading into town, and it's fair to say at this point that I was definitely in a mood.

No answers, just more questions – Aunt Cass giving me instructions without handing over information with it. Having a teenager snark at me sealed the deal. So I decided to play the silence game until Kira cracked.

We were on the edge of Harlot Bay when Kira finally started talking.

"Your aunt is way cooler than my grandma," she said, examining the three beacons. She ran her fingers over the soft black feathers before picking one up and brushing it against her face.

It was so cute I cracked immediately.

"Sometimes she is. She cursed Molly to only say nice things about her a while back."

"She actually curses people? My grandmother is all about

control, control, control. She doesn't let us use magic for *anything*."

That matched up pretty closely with what I knew about Hattie Stern. I'd been going to her for training to learn how to control the power to pull heat or cold out of anything. It had first happened by accident when I'd helped Aunt Cass put out the cottage fire using ocean water. I'd quickly discovered the power was incredibly addictive. The first time I'd been in training with Hattie and reached out my hand to pull some heat from a kettle, she'd whacked me across the back of the knuckles with a wooden ruler.

I'd finished my training with her only recently and was looking forward to *never* going back.

"Sounds like she lives up to her last name," I said.

We kept driving, going somewhat slower now thanks to the summer traffic. It was pretty much peak vacation season, and tourists had flooded Harlot Bay, filling up all the hotels and motels and all the campsites over on Truer Island.

Since the lighthouse fire, the lighthouse had been blocked off to tourists because it was considered structurally unsound. Tourists still visited, though, because the lighthouse was still listed in all the guidebooks. I was hoping we'd get enough privacy to set up the beacon.

I took a detour to bypass the main part of town, which would have so many tourists crossing the street it would be virtually at a standstill. This took us along the Esplanade so we could look out on the pristine sands and calm Harlot Bay. The beach was filled with swimming and sunbathing tourists, and I saw Kira glancing more than once at cute teenage boys.

"Do you want to go to beach later?" I asked.

Kira immediately looked away from a particularly cute group of boys who were throwing a ball around and wrestling with each other.

"Maybe, I don't know," she said, looking down at her lap.

I didn't push it. I didn't have the whole story, or really *any* of the story, but given that she was a Slip Witch and a teenager, I knew what she was going through. Aunt Cass had helped train me when I was a teenager so I could find ways to control most of my powers (or survive them without too much trouble).

"I'm a Slip Witch too, you know. So is Aunt Cass."

This was obviously the wrong approach. Kira frowned and pulled out her phone, tapping away on it. We drove in silence the rest of the way out to the lighthouse and parked in the almost-empty parking lot.

"Okay, time for the first beacon," I said.

I took a look at the instructions Aunt Cass had given me. The biggest one, written in bold with multiple exclamation marks after it, was: PUT THEM UP SOMEWHERE HIGH!!!!!!!

Together we walked up to the lighthouse and skipped under the string of warning flags surrounding it. There were two other cars in the parking lot, but there was no one around. They must have walked down the cliff steps to the beach.

The door to the lighthouse was blackened and warped but still intact. It was chained shut and there was a thick padlock attached to it.

"How do we get in?" Kira asked.

"Like this," I said, and cast an unlocking spell. The lock opened and I swiftly removed it and loosened the chain so I could open the door.

"My grandma was right about the Torrents. You really don't care when you use magic, do you?" Kira said. There was a little bit of attitude in it, but I got the distinct feeling that it wasn't from her.

"If Slip Witches don't use their power, it comes out in

other ways. That's lesson one," I said and went through the door. Kira followed me in.

The interior of the lighthouse was burned black from the fire that had been set by Jason Greenway, the husband of the couple who'd murdered Kyle and Holly Morella. He'd burned the lighthouse down in an attempt to kill me, apparently in some hope that he could stop me from investigating the skeletons that had been found out on Truer Island. But the idiot hadn't realized the investigation was going ahead whether I wrote any articles about it or not. The halfwit had even attacked Carter Wilkins and another man behind the soundstage at the Festival of Lights, as though if he could somehow debilitate both reporters in town he'd get away with murder.

"The stairs are broken. How are we supposed to get the beacon up to the top?" Kira asked.

During the fire, the stairs that led to the top of the lighthouse had collapsed. Someone must have removed the wreckage, though.

"Do you know how to do a levitation spell?" I asked her.

"Um, sort of. Not really allowed to use magic for no reason at home."

"You're not at home anymore. You're living with the Torrents, and we use magic for any reason we want."

"Where am I levitating it to?" Kira asked.

I pointed up to the highest window, which had a ledge a few inches wide below it.

"If you floated it up there, no one would be able to get it down easily, even if they could see it. Since the stairs are out, I'd say it would probably stay hidden up there for a long time."

Kira took out the beacon and held it in the palm of the hand. I could see her working herself up to using her magic. She took three quick breaths and I felt the magic around us ripple. The beacon floated up out of her hand and began to slowly make its way up.

She got it about halfway up before the magic started to jerk.

Kira was biting her lip in anxiety and looking at the beacon as though she could push it up to the windowsill by sheer force of will. That's not entirely too far off when it comes to magic, but she needed to learn to relax as well – squeezing too hard can cut you off from the source of the power.

I stepped closer to her and touched her on the shoulder, then took a slow breath myself.

"You got this," I said, giving the beacon a bit of a nudge myself.

The beacon floated upwards. It quickly reached the window, where Kira slowed it down and then landed it on the sill, incredibly gently. Once it was in place, she let the magic go and turned to me, grinning.

"I did it!" she said and then held out her hand for a high five.

I slapped her palm.

"Good job. Let's set up the others," I said.

On the way back to the car, Kira started chattering away about how amazing it was to lift the beacon up onto the shelf. Since the ban on magic at her house was pretty much complete, she was probably feeling giddy after having used her magic properly for the first time in ages.

The second stop was an address high up in the hills of the rich district. We drove over there and found an empty parcel of land with a lone tree growing on it. This was a little trickier. I had to cast a concealment spell on both of us, and then Kira floated the beacon up to nestle in the hollow of the tree high above us.

She landed it perfectly, grinning as she did.

We talked as we drove around and I made sure to keep it light, not saying a single word about Hattie Stern or why Kira had come to stay with us. She was very excited about floating the two beacons up to put them in place, and I got the feeling she was treated like a child back at home.

"So can I do whatever magic I want at your house?" Kira asked me as we approached the final location.

"Depends what it is. We don't do any magic to harm anyone else, and we keep it secret. We don't have a ban on it. My mother and aunts have put love potions in cakes before."

"Wow," Kira said.

She went *very quiet* then, and I could almost see the gears turning in her head. Was this what it was like when I was a teenager? Was it possible the moms knew exactly what was going on but had to maintain a front of always nipping at our heels?

"Love potion love isn't really great love," I said as I turned onto the final street.

"Oh."

"It can grow to be real love, but who wants to start with fake love?"

I left out that plenty of witches were quite happy to start with fake love.

The final location was... a creepy murder house. It was clearly abandoned. The windows were broken, the yard full of dying weeds and the paint was flaking.

It was three stories tall, with an epic spire at the top. I looked at Aunt Cass's note.

ON THE SPIRE!

"Too high for levitation," I said.

I cast a quick concealment spell on us while we were still in the car in case any nosy neighbors were watching. The tug of the spell was slight – like carrying a heavy bag around.

"Is this a haunted house?" Kira asked.

"Looks creepy, but I'm guessing no."

We went to the front door, which was hanging ajar. It creaked as I pushed it open.

"Super creepshow," Kira whispered.

"It's fine. Just an empty house. Let's get up the stairs and see if we can find a way to get the beacon to the top."

I left the door ajar… not for any reason, really.

Okay, in case we had to run for our lives.

We went up the creaky stairs to the third floor, both of us trying not to look in the rooms but seeing all kinds of horror movie stuff anyway. An empty crib. An old rocking horse sitting in the middle of a room. Some children's shoes.

At the top of the stairs, we found a door that led to an outdoor rooftop garden. Unlike the rest of the house, it was still in good condition. There were some very comfortable-looking wicker chairs and a few long planter boxes full of flowers.

Kira floated the beacon up without warning me, so I had to cast a very hasty concealment spell over it. A minute more and the beacon was in place atop the spire.

"Let's get out of here, before some guy who's wearing his mother's skin as a suit comes to kill us," Kira said, her hands on her hips.

"Good idea," I said, seeing a glimmer of something ghostly down in the backyard. It looked like a woman. Did I tell you not *all* ghosts are friendly?

We rushed out of there and back to the car.

On the way home, Kira retreated to the safety of her phone, tapping away in a steady stream. For my part, I was seeing that perhaps she wasn't just a spiky, annoying teenager. I mean, yes, she was *that*, but she was also funny and interesting.

We arrived back at Torrent Mansion to find Aunt Cass waiting for us.

"Okay, teenage Slip Witch, you're with me now. Not you, though," she said. She waved at Kira to follow her into the mansion.

As soon as Aunt Cass turned her back, I poked out my tongue at her. Kira stifled a laugh and then followed Aunt Cass inside.

I went back to our end of the mansion alone and rode out the rest of Sunday doing not much at all.

Well, that's not entirely true. I'd managed to distract myself all morning from the fact that a special arson investigator was in town and wanted to interview me, but alone for the rest of Sunday, I had plenty of time to dwell on how many million years I was going to spend in jail.

I tried to tell myself I was innocent (I was, of course) but I still couldn't shake the feeling that something bad was going to happen.

CHAPTER FIVE

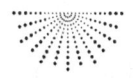

The big question of Monday morning was: where did I go wrong?

I was sitting in my office, having a good old-fashioned misery wallow rather than working.

The *Harlot Bay Reader* was only ever viable with free rent, and it never really made anything coming close to a full-time job, but at least the money had been on an upward trajectory – that was, until I was frozen for six weeks. I'd been working hard to revive it, posting articles day and night and writing about everything and anything but that break was a wound my poor website simply couldn't recover from.

The *where did I go wrong* in that case was: living in a small tourist town where not much happens AND being frozen for six weeks.

I was still trying to help John Smith move on, but that only brought in about forty bucks a week (sometimes more if he forgot we'd already had a session and left extra money on the desk for me).

Essentially, I was starting to delve into new and exciting levels of poverty. The moms had been throwing me some work at Big Pie (two bucks an hour above minimum wage, woo-hoo!) but even they couldn't give me a full-time job without firing someone else (which would never happen). I knew I should stop buying my lunch, but it was seriously starting to be the one and only small joy I had left.

So here I was in the office, playing the what-do-I-want-to-do-with-my-life game.

Not a fun game.

I was staring at nothing, moving around thoughts of living in a seaside town, poverty, fires, witches, and seemingly everything else that was going wrong in my life, when there came a tentative knock at the door.

The door was ajar and swung open to reveal a small man in his fifties. He was thin and pale – definitely a tourist and not from Harlot Bay.

"Excuse me… I thought this was the *Harlot Bay Times?*"

"Sorry, this is the *Harlot Bay Reader*. We are an online newspaper."

I don't know why I said *we are* – it was just me sitting in the office. It wasn't like I had some staff hidden away somewhere.

"Can I still place a death notice?"

"Ah… sure. Let me take down some details. Please come in, sit down."

The man shuffled past me, seeming deflated and apologetic in every movement. He sat down on the sofa. I grabbed a notepad and paper.

"I'm Harlow Torrent, by the way."

"Henry Gray. I'm—" He gave an enormous yawn and then rubbed his eyes. They were red-rimmed.

"Sorry, came down from New York. I've been traveling for a solid day. My mother, Lenora, she died in a house fire."

"I'm so sorry," I said. The more I looked at Henry, the more I realized he was completely exhausted. I got the feeling if he closed his eyes, he would fall asleep on my sofa.

"Thank you," Henry murmured.

"I saw the fire," I said, and then mentally kicked myself. What was I going to do? Describe how I'd seen the fire that had killed his mother?

"The police said it was quite extreme. They're still investigating. I can't go into the house because it's not structurally safe." Henry sighed and looked at the floor. A tear trickled down his nose, which he quickly wiped away.

"My mother was old, slipping into Alzheimer's, and we kept saying we'd come down here to find a good retirement home for her and put the house on the market. We just couldn't find the time. Now it looks like she left something on the stove and burnt the house down."

I was sitting there with my pen on the pad, not writing anything. This was more of a confession than a funeral notice.

"Did the fire department tell you it was something left on the stove?" I asked.

Henry shook his head and rubbed his eyes again.

"No, we're guessing. Apparently it's very common for people with Alzheimer's to die that way. I guess it could have been an accident."

"It could be. A lot of those old houses had old wiring in them," I said.

I knew I shouldn't be speculating, but he just seemed so broken and crushed by the guilt and I didn't want him to feel so bad. Although it would only be a short-term solution. Perhaps the fire department *would* find she'd left something on the stove, and then he would have to live with the fact that because he couldn't find the time to visit his mother, an elderly slip had resulted in her death.

"What do you want me to write in the notice?" I asked.

"Funeral notice for Lenora Gray. Thursday at the Three Pines Chapel at eleven a.m. Dearly beloved mother of two and grandmother of six. You will be in our hearts forever."

I wrote this down, feeling tears begin to spike in the corner of my eyes. I'd put it up on my online newspaper, but I had to make sure Carter printed it as well. Given how few people were visiting the *Harlot Bay Reader*, if it was only me running the notice, it was highly likely no one would attend the funeral.

"I'll make sure this gets into the *Harlot Bay Times* too," I said.

"What do I owe you?"

"No charge."

"Thanks," Henry said and stood up.

He paused at the door.

"I know this is going to sound bad. We need a real estate agent to sell the land, to put it on the market. That and the empty parcel next to it. Do you know who I should talk to? We want to have the funeral and get it done as soon as possible."

Immediately Dominic Gresso flashed to my mind. There were a few real estate agents in town, but he was the most well-known. There was another one, Sylvester Coldwell, who I would say was probably the sleaziest real estate developer around, even worse than Dominic and that's saying something. But it wasn't my place to judge...

I wrote down Dominic's and Sylvester's details and gave them to Henry.

"Thanks for this," Henry said before he left.

I called the *Harlot Bay Times*. Carter answered the phone.

"I need to place a death notice," I told him.

"Why aren't you doing it in your own newspaper?" he asked. I could practically hear the quote marks around "newspaper."

I ignored his jab.

"It's for Lenora Gray."

I read out the funeral notification as Henry had given it to me. When I finished, Carter told me it would cost twenty-five dollars.

"Okay, fine, I'll come by at lunchtime and pay. Make sure it goes in tomorrow's issue."

"Why are you placing the death notice for Lenora Gray? Did you meet her son?"

Part of me wanted to tell Carter that, yes, I had met Henry, just to rub it in that he wasn't the only journalist in town and I'd gotten the jump on him yet again. The other part wanted to tell him nothing for the rest of his life. He'd always been a stickler for the truth and facts, but it seemed that modern economic pressure was working on Carter as well, and his newspaper was increasingly being filled with speculation and outright lies written as questions. *Corruption in the Police Force? Poison Dumped in the Water? Dogs Running Amok?* Not to mention he'd written quite a few things that were untrue about me and my family.

"I have nothing more to add, Carter. It's just a death notice. Please don't write an article about it."

The phone was silent for a moment and then Carter cleared his throat.

"I guess they're going for a quick real estate sale?"

"What makes you say that?"

"Old lady, family doesn't live here… common story. The kids are going to put the property on the market and sell it as fast as they possibly can."

"I really wouldn't know," I lied.

"Seems that whoever buys the property at fire sale prices, excuse the phrase, is probably going to benefit. If you want to be a journalist, Harlow, you need to think beyond the surface layer," he said. I went to retort, but Carter had hung up. That didn't stop me, however.

"Shut up, you arrogant buffoon!" I said to the phone in my hand.

"There's a headline! Local reporter yells at someone!" a voice from behind me said. I whirled around to find myself facing Sylvester Coldwell, the sleazy real estate agent I'd been thinking bad thoughts about only about ten minutes earlier.

Was this some crazy new Slip Witch power? I just had to think about someone and they would show up?

Jack, Jack, Jack.

He didn't appear.

Sylvester was tall with light hair and blue eyes. He'd actually be good-looking if he didn't exude a persistent reeking sleaziness.

"Hi, Mr. Coldwell, how can I help you?" I said, quickly recovering my equilibrium.

"I came up here to see how our local tax dollars are being spent with the free rent and all. Is it only you who works in your business?"

"That's right. Just me."

"How much money are you making?"

"That would be private."

Sylvester looked around my office which, honestly, wasn't that clean. There were two coffee mugs left sitting out and a few pieces of note paper strewn about the place.

"How well do you think Bishop Developments downstairs is doing? Is it creating revenue for the town?"

"I have no idea. Why are you asking?"

Sylvester took another look around the office, as if assessing every single part of it.

"This place has good bones," he said.

"I like it."

"I'm sure you do. Free rent courtesy of the taxpayer to run your business. If only we could all be that lucky."

"What you mean? The free rent is to encourage more small businesses to start. That's something Harlot Bay needs."

"I'm sure those businesses getting free rent say that a lot," Sylvester said. "I have to go now."

"Whatever," I said, channeling my teenage self, or possibly Kira.

"See if you talk like that when I get this stupid program shut down," Sylvester snapped. He turned away for a moment and then back again, giving me a greasy smile.

"I apologize. I didn't mean that. Some of us taxpayers are worried about where our money is being spent. I actually came here because I want to talk to your family about buying and developing Torrent Mansion. Do you think they would be interested?"

He pulled a business card out of his wallet and held it out to me. I felt like screaming at him to get his sleaziness out of my face.

I pulled myself together.

"We're not interested in selling," I said through gritted teeth.

"I haven't seen April Torrent around for a while. Do you think it's possible I could meet with her?"

"She doesn't meet real estate agents. Now I need to get back to work, so could you please go?"

Seeing that I wasn't going to take the business card, Sylvester put it down on the desk before seeing himself out. I heard the stairs creaking as he walked down to Jonas's office and knocked on the door. I listened to the two of them talking while I stood there waiting for my blood to stop boiling.

As if I didn't have enough problems. The mayor's free

rent program had faced some opposition from local businesses who felt that it was unfair for *them* to be paying rent and a new business not to pay anything. The mayor had won them over, however. The fact was that empty buildings didn't help business. It was a bad sign as well, especially when some of the local teenagers broke windows and started vandalizing the places. Eventually the business owners had reluctantly come around, and as a result some of the empty buildings now had people like me trying to work and start businesses. The good side effect was that none of the buildings had been vandalized in quite a while. Now it appeared that Sylvester Coldwell was intent on pushing the issue again.

And what was with these real estate agents who wanted to buy Torrent Mansion and develop it? The place had been a wreck for a *very* long time. The moms put some money into it and started a bed-and-breakfast, and the next minute it's a prime development opportunity?

And what was with Carter Wilkins and his "this is how you be a real journalist" garbage? I was the one who'd tracked down Preston Jacobs! I was the one who'd found two murderers!

Like *he'd* broken any big scandals in Harlot Bay with his cutting-edge journalism.

But although I was angry and really wished I'd told Carter to shut up, he did have a point about Lenora Gray. It was common practice that, when an elderly resident passed away, the children who inherited the home put it up for quick sale. Often houses were sold completely furnished with only minor personal effects being removed because the kids couldn't be bothered with removing all the furniture.

Was Carter suggesting that the fire that'd killed Lenora Gray was set deliberately? It seemed such a roundabout way to acquire her land. Especially given that Henry would just put the house on the open market. Would the person who supposedly started the fire hope to get in first?

I was back at my desk, chewing this over in my mind, and also the problem that two real estate agents wanted to meet in person with my frozen grandmother, when Mom called.

"…going to need sixteen boxes. Harlow, good, you finally answered," Mom said.

"You only just called," I protested.

Mom ignored this. She had a habit of pretending every time she called that this was actually call number twenty-five and I hadn't answered any of the previous ones. Then *finally* she had gotten through to me.

"Is Kira Stern with you?" she asked.

I knew immediately that something was going on. But I didn't have enough information to know whether I should lie and say she was, or say she wasn't and possibly uncover that Kira had lied at some point.

"I haven't seen her today," I said, hedging my bets.

"She's going to be doing some work, either here at Big Pie, with your cousins, or with you. We'll discuss it tonight after our big announcement."

"What big announcement?"

"It's a surprise. Having a family dinner tonight. There are no guests, so it's family and Kira. Make sure you're on time."

"When have I *not* been on time?"

Mom ignored that too.

"Going to need you to do some work at the bakery this week. Is that okay?"

I glanced at my computer, where I'd written the first three sentences about the ongoing foreshore restoration project.

"That's fine," I said. "See you tonight."

The phone went dead in my ear before I could even say goodbye.

A big announcement? The last time there had been a big announcement, the moms had entered us into the Gold Mud Run. Hopefully it wasn't on a level with that, although given that they'd all been away at a business seminar over the weekend, perhaps they'd come up with some crazy new idea to make money. Which wouldn't be such a bad thing, really. The Torrent Mansion Bed-and-Breakfast had been full most Friday and Saturday nights, but for some reason people didn't book very much during the week.

I called Molly to see if she knew anything about the announcement, but she didn't answer. Even after hiring staff to help them at Traveler, they were still rushed off their feet.

I checked the time, but it was barely past ten in the morning. Far too early to go to Traveler to see my cousins on a lunch break. I decided to use the last two hours before lunch to do some journalism work.

Yes, I was essentially working out of spite, even though Carter Wilkins wouldn't know it. I was going to find out what was behind these fires.

Although Aunt Cass said she thought it had been a fire spirit, perhaps people were involved too.

I dived into the history of fires in Harlot Bay, and soon the world faded away.

CHAPTER SIX

Molly looked like she was about to kill someone.

She and Luce were standing across the street from Traveler, having a conversation with a man and woman. It was very clear even from a distance that Molly was definitely *not* enjoying said conversation. She was smiling at them through gritted teeth. Luce had plastered on a smile as well and she had a glassy look in her eyes. As I approached, Molly glanced at me and flashed the *help me* eyes.

"We're really not interested in selling. Not for any amount of money," Molly said, clearly repeating herself.

"Not even twenty thousand?" the man said.

"Not even for twenty thousand."

"Hey, guys, ready to go for lunch?" I asked.

"We are! Sorry, we have to go now. Good luck," Molly said to the couple.

"I really think we can do some business together," the woman said.

"We can't and we won't," Molly said. She turned her back

on the couple and walked away, a little down the street. Luce and I followed.

The couple went the other way, muttering between themselves.

As soon as we were out of earshot, Molly swore and stomped her feet.

"What was that about?"

"They want to buy Stefano," Luce said. "But we're not interested."

"Stefano?"

"The coffee machine," Molly said in between stomping her feet a few more times.

"Love you, Stefano!" Luce said and blew a kiss in Traveler's general direction.

The line for coffees was out the door. There was a double-decker bus parked down the street. Inside Traveler, Molly and Luce's three new staff members, Alex, Isabella, and Julie, were working frantically behind the counter.

"Are you sure we can go for lunch? It looks crazy in there," I asked.

"We've trained them as much as we can, and at some point we have to be able to leave Traveler. Today is that day," Luce said.

"Why do those people want to buy Stefano?" I asked.

Molly made a snorting sound.

"They're planning on opening a coffee shop. At first I thought they were just interested in information about the coffee machine. But then they kept asking a lot of questions about where we got it from, who was the supplier, all that kind of thing. I told them the website we brought it from, not that they had any others for sale."

"Twenty thousand dollars is a lot of money, though," I said.

"It *is* a lot of money, but we'll be making far more than that in only a couple of months with this crazy coffee."

We hadn't made a proper plan for lunch, but in our wandering away from Traveler, we ended up in front of Five Slices, a pizza place. We went inside and sat in a booth.

"Mom told me that they have a big announcement tonight. Any idea what it is?" I asked.

Molly and Luce pulled out their phones and read the messages that they had received from their mothers.

"Mine says, 'Big surprise, dinnertime, dress well,'" Molly said, a glint of fire in her eye.

"Mine is... the same," Luce said. She didn't want to get Molly all worked up. Last time that happened, Molly had gone to dinner in a slinky low-cut tight dress just to annoy her mother.

"I don't like it when they have big announcements," I said.

"It probably has something to do with the bed-and-breakfast," Luce said. "They did go to that seminar thing."

"Okay, well, I think we have bigger problems," I said.

I told them about Sylvester Coldwell coming to my office and asking questions about Grandma April and how he wanted to buy and develop Torrent Mansion.

"Two real estate agents want to develop the mansion? It's not that popular, is it?" Luce said.

"I guess maybe they're seeing the potential?" Molly said.

"You both missing the point. They're trying to get in contact with Grandma, who is currently frozen in the basement and is not going to speak to them at all. Dominic Gresso said he had investigators on the case. What if it gets out that no one has seen Grandma for the last twenty years?"

"I'm sure Aunt Cass and the moms have it under control," Luce said, although she kept fiddling with her menu, a sure sign of nerves.

We were interrupted by Sasha, the waitress, who took our

orders. Five slices only served five types of pizza sold by the slice. I ordered a slice of margherita, a slice of pepperoni and a soda (sorry, thighs).

"All we can do is tell them tonight at dinner about the real estate agents. I'm sure they'll come up with something," Molly said.

I sat back in the booth and looked through the one menu Sasha had left on the table. Clearly my cousins weren't taking this as seriously as I was. I felt a little annoyed, but then on the other hand, perhaps I was just worked up. After all, they weren't the ones facing investigation. A problem which, I might note, no one had really talked about or seemed interested in. Both of them had gotten so wrapped up in their business and their new boyfriends that they really didn't seem to care much that an arson investigator had come to the house to ask questions about me.

I pushed these quite sour thoughts out of my mind and listened in as Molly and Luce started talking about making plans for the weekend. They were both going out with their boyfriends to do all the fun, exciting things you can do around Harlot Bay.

"We're all thinking of going to the beach on Sunday. Do you want to come?" Luce asked.

"Yeah, maybe," I said, noncommittally.

Molly must have sensed something was wrong.

"You okay?" she asked.

"Preoccupied with work, I guess. Carter Wilkins implied that I wasn't a 'real journalist' earlier today, so I've been investigating fires around Harlot Bay. Seems like there have been quite a few going back over the last hundred years."

"So do you think the fires were lit by an arsonist?" Molly asked. "Aunt Cass seems to believe it's a fire spirit."

"What?" I said. Aunt Cass had sworn me to secrecy about

her room downstairs, and then she'd told Molly and Luce anyway?

"Yeah, she said it's a fire spirit and that you and Kira had been setting up beacons for her. Do you think she's going to catch it?" Luce asked.

"Maybe. We set up the beacons, so I guess we'll see. Did Aunt Cass tell you she has a complete laboratory underground, too?" I said.

"Really? What does she do down there?" Molly asked.

I realized my error far too late. I was feeling a little snarky towards Aunt Cass because she had sworn me secrecy for apparently no reason, and so I'd let out that she had a laboratory under the house. Since Aunt Cass had cursed Molly, she'd had been looking for a way to get back at her. She had taken the "revenge is a dish best served cold" approach and had been biding her time. Now I'd just handed her something she could use on a silver platter.

"It's no big deal. Actually, it was just a table with a few things that she used to make that potion to protect us against the morchint. I think she got rid of it all."

"Liar, liar, pants on fire," Molly stated. "She had all that glassware delivered, and I know she's had other packages showing up at the house. Now we just have to work out how to use this information."

I felt a sudden panic bubbling in my stomach. If Aunt Cass found out I'd blabbed about her underground lab, there was sure to be trouble.

"Or perhaps you could just leave it be and leave her alone. I think she enjoys all the conflict, anyway. By engaging with her and trying to use this to your advantage, she is probably going to win in some other way," I said as Sasha delivered our pizza and drinks. I took the opportunity to eat rather than talk.

"Yeah, maybe you're right," Molly said.

I didn't believe she was backing off this for one second.

We quickly changed topics after that, moving on to the renovation plans Molly and Luce had for Traveler. They'd finally come to an agreement and decided to transform it into a full coffee shop. Because they were so busy during the day, they'd have builders coming in late in the afternoon and working into the evening, trying to do the renovation in stages.

"But no matter what, we're going to have to shut down for a day or two," Luce explained.

"I can't wait to see it," I said.

It was good to hang out with my cousins, and I was definitely happy for their success... although it did seem like everyone else's lives were on an upward trajectory and mine was spiraling down to the ground. Their business was thriving and now they were expanding. The moms had the bakery and the Torrent Mansion Bed-and-Breakfast. Aunt Cass was training Kira and I'm sure had some other sneaky source of income hidden away.

And what was I doing? Investigating fires over the last hundred years in Harlot Bay, worrying about being charged with arson and trying to help a ghost who didn't remember anything to move on. Oh, and every week I was writing a letter to a possible future boyfriend who still hadn't returned.

"Who's that guy out there?" Luce asked, nodding out the window.

I turned around my seat see a guy in bright orange shorts and a Hawaiian shirt standing across the road. He looked sunburned and had a camera around his neck.

"Just a tourist? Why?"

"I saw him a few days ago outside Traveler. And then I think he followed us here," Luce said.

I turned around again for a proper look out the window.

The man was checking his camera. He looked up at the pizza shop, checked his camera again and then wandered off down the street, taking photos of a few of the buildings.

"I'm pretty sure he's just a tourist," I said.

I mostly said that because I didn't really want to deal with the idea that someone else was following me or my cousins! We finished our lunch, and Molly and Luce returned to Traveler. Despite wanting to go home and sleep the rest of my life away, I went back to the office. I was there for maybe forty-five minutes, struggling through some newspaper article I didn't care about, before I finally did give up and drove home.

CHAPTER SEVEN

Adams was waiting for me when I got home. I picked him up and he snuggled into me.

"Why do you smell like an old lady's sock drawer?" I asked him.

"No, I don't," Adams said, purring.

He really did, though. It was like he'd spent the morning rolling around in lavender. After a while I wandered off to my bedroom with the intention of having a short nap. I know this was no way to deal with all of my problems... but on the other hand, my bed was *very* comfy and the room was cool.

I woke up when Molly and Luce got home. It was very late in the afternoon. I sleepily made my way out of the kitchen and then, because I wasn't quick enough, I had to be third in line to have a shower to get ready for dinner. While Molly was showering, Luce told me in an undertone that the couple had come back again, this time offering thirty thousand to buy the coffee machine.

"So no talk about the coffee machine. I think she's going to kill anyone who says anything about it," Luce told me.

"I promise," I said. Once we were ready, we walked down to the main house and into the dining room. The moms were in the kitchen doing the usual talking/bickering/meddling thing. I heard my name, but then they must have heard us, because the talking subsided.

I grabbed Molly and Luce and quickly pulled them into the lounge.

"They're meddling! Did you hear Mom say my name?" I asked.

"Dude, you're going crazy," Molly said.

"Maybe you need to have a glass of wine?" Luce added.

I took a deep breath and tried to steady myself. Okay, so they were a bit right. Just because I'd heard my name didn't mean anything was happening.

"Okay, get the wine," I said. We returned to the dining room just as Mom emerged from the kitchen carrying a covered serving tray.

"Oh, good, you're all here," she said, smiling at us.

I saw Molly and Luce glance at each other. Yes, Mom is generally cheerful, but this cheerfulness had an underlying sneakiness... she was planning something.

We took our seats at the table after Molly retrieved a bottle of white wine.

"Has anyone seen Aunt Cass and Kira?" Mom asked.

"Nope," Molly said and then took big gulp of wine. Luce shook her head and followed suit.

"Not me," I said and took a mouthful myself. I felt the alcohol hit my stomach in a warm rush and a moment later started to relax. Yes, I was possibly under investigation for arson and, yes, my business was failing and, no, I had zero reasons to think anything would change, but did that matter all that much? Jack had sent me a letter saying he was coming back soon. Eventually I would see his handsome face again. Who cared what Carter thought of my journalism skills? The guy was one step above reporting on "Mysterious Mud Monster Found in Harlot Bay!"

Aunt Freya and Aunt Ro emerged from the kitchen carrying more covered serving dishes and brought them out to the table. The moms shuttled back and forth bringing out plates and silverware and even more covered dishes. It seemed they'd really gone all out for this dinner. I sat there drinking my wine, listening to Luce and Molly chat about their business plans for when the renovations were to be done. They had a local architect drawing up plans for the interior layout.

As I sat there, I felt more relaxed with each passing minute (thanks white wine!). Since the Torrent Mansion Bed-and-Breakfast had opened, we'd often had visitors sitting at our dinner table in the morning and at night. I'm not sure the moms had entirely anticipated this happening. As a result, we hadn't had many dinners where it was just us witches.

Despite being peak vacation season, there were no bookings for the next few days. I expected the moms would be trying to pull us into dinners at every opportunity they got.

Finally, they finished ferrying dishes out of the kitchen. They brought a few more bottles of wine and then sat down across from us.

Aunt Ro checked her watch.

"So unlike Aunt Cass to miss dinner," she said a touch sarcastically. Aunt Freya and Mom laughed, but then quickly stifled that when they heard a door slamming in the kitchen. Aunt Cass and Kira must've been somewhere under the house, probably down in Aunt Cass's investigation room or the mad scientist's laboratory that I'd told Molly and Luce about.

Mom had just lifted the lid on a spectacular-looking roast chicken when Aunt Cass and Kira walked in from the kitchen. There was a collective gasp from the other side of the table, and Mom dropped the silver serving dish lid on the table with a gigantic clang.

Kira still had a pink streak through her hair and a silver nose piercing ring. Standing beside her, Aunt Cass now had a pink streak through her hair and a shiny silver nose ring.

There was a pregnant pause before Aunt Cass turned to Kira and said, "Wow, awkward much?"

Kira laughed and then they high-fived.

Yes, you heard that correctly. The sixteen-year-old pink-haired nose-pierced Slip Witch and possible Queen of Sarcasm high-fived our somewhere-in-her-eighties great-aunt, who now had a vivid pink streak in her hair and a shiny silver nose piercing.

Aunt Cass made her way around to her traditional position at the head of the table and then waved at the three of us to move down to make room for Kira. We did so happily. Aunt Cass grabbed one of the bottles of wine and quickly filled her glass. It was when she reached for Kira's glass that Mom finally spoke up.

"Um... we... it's not right to... we don't give wine to children," she finally said.

"I know we don't give wine to children. There are no children here," Aunt Cass replied, bottle in hand.

Kira, who had been grinning, suddenly appeared panicked.

Welcome to your first Torrent dinner, kid.

"It's okay. I don't really like wine much anyway," she said. Mom and Aunt Cass stared off at each other for a moment before Aunt Cass put the bottle down.

"Okay, dinner, everybody," Mom said weakly. They removed the covers on the rest the dishes to reveal a spread of gloriously delicious food. Roast potatoes, roast carrots, roast pumpkin with pieces of roasted garlic. There were steamed green beans with almond slivers, a salad that had strawberries in it, and another salad with various sliced mushrooms.

But all the deliciousness spread in front of us wasn't enough to get us to ignore Aunt Cass's new look. Years ago, the three of us had wanted to get nose piercings and somehow the moms had found out. They'd ganged up on us and used everything in their power to try to stop us. At the time, Aunt Cass had backed them up!

We'd gone ahead anyway, but after only a week or two we'd taken them out. They'd essentially been ruined by our meddling family. And now we were here, with Aunt Cass having a pink streak in her hair and a silver nose piercing herself. None of us were going to let *that* slide.

"What's the phrase I'm thinking of, Aunt Cass?" Molly began sweetly. "It was something to do with piercings and how they look on young girls. Can you help me out?"

"Silver piercings look amazing?" Aunt Cass said, filling up her plate with green beans.

"No, that wasn't it," Luce said.

"I feel like it was something negative, something to discourage young witches from getting nose piercings. That was right, wasn't it, Mom?" I said.

The moms were obviously still flabbergasted by Aunt Cass's new look. Aunt Freya was frantically serving herself food and not looking at anyone, Aunt Ro had drunk a glass of wine and was now working on a second, and Mom was sitting there with an empty plate and a stunned look on her face.

"What? Sorry, what did you say?" Mom stuttered.

"I said –"

"So what's the big announcement?" Aunt Cass said, cutting me off.

"Oh, yes, well, we have a lot of exciting news," Mom began, grabbing that distraction.

Molly leapt up from the table, banging her legs against it and making the silverware jump. Kira looked at me with a panicked expression on her face. Under the devilish influence of wine, I gave her a devilish wink.

Molly brought her finger down from the sky above like she was pointing out a murderer and pointed it right at Aunt Cass.

"You said we couldn't get nose piercings because they looked terrible and they weren't suitable for young witches!"

She swung her accusing finger around to her mom, Aunt Ro.

"You said even worse things! You said we'd end up joining some kind of heavy metal death cult!"

Luce leapt up from her chair and pointed her finger at her mom, Aunt Freya.

"You forbade me to get a nose piercing. Forbade me!"

Not one to miss out on all the fun, I jumped out of my chair. Thanks to the wine, I bashed my legs quite hard against the table.

"Ow!" I said, pointing my finger at Mom.

The moms were about to retort when a napkin next to the salad bowl burst into flames.

"Sorry!" Kira yelped.

Aunt Cass put her hand on top of Kira's.

"Remember what I told you. Take a deep breath, center yourself," she said.

Another napkin burst into flames, but no one reached out to put it out. The same thing had happened to me when I was a teenager and I got stressed.

Kira took two quick, shuddering breaths and then managed to control herself. She took one long, slow breath, held it for a moment and then let it out steadily. She stretched out her hand towards the burning napkins, fingers splayed, and then closed them into a fist. The fire was extinguished instantly.

Then she grinned and looked at the six of us.

"I did it!"

We all erupted in cheers, the nose-piercing, pink-hair-dyeing incident forgotten for the time being. Luce grabbed Kira and hugged her, the teenage girl wearing a goofy smile. Everyone sat down and resumed dinner, digging into the delicious food. After a few minutes of witches eating and drinking and moaning at how delicious the food was, Aunt Cass repeated her question.

"What are these big announcements?" she asked, pointing her fork at Mom.

Mom likes to make a show of things. She dinged her wineglass like we were at a wedding, even though we were all sitting there paying attention.

"Well, firstly, we would like to announce that the renovations of Torrent Mansion are complete for the time being."

"Woo-hoo!" Molly said and raised a glass. We all said cheers to that, Kira tapping her glass of mineral water against our wineglasses.

"We have six fully furnished bedrooms now. We'll rent them out again now that the website is upgraded. It was having a problem where it wouldn't let people book on weekdays," Aunt Ro said.

"The other big news is that next weekend, we're all participating in the pirate parade. We're going to be building a float together. Isn't that exciting!" Aunt Freya said.

She must've seen the sudden glassy smiles facing her from the other side of the table.

The pirate parade is a yearly tradition in Harlot Bay, celebrating the bloodthirsty murderous pirates that sailed up and down this part of the Atlantic. We honor these criminals in the best way possible: a giant parade of floats, all kinds of food and fun and games for the little children.

Of course everyone knows the biggest and baddest pirate in this area was Blackbeard, so many adults and kids dress up as that crazy pirate.

We've attended many times in the past, but never really participated. The pirate parade is in the summer, so it's usually a hot, sweaty affair under the sweltering sun.

"We have plans," Molly said quickly.

"No, you don't," Aunt Ro said.

"We do. We're going... spelunking," Luce said.

Spelunking?

"No, you're all coming to the pirate parade and that's final," Aunt Freya snapped.

Molly and Luce turned to me, but I didn't have anything to add. My mind went blank.

"Okay, fine..." I said, defeated.

"Excellent. We'll arrange the costumes. During the week you can help work on the float," Mom said.

We continued on with dinner, the conversation switching back to the Torrent Mansion renovations ending and the new website. The moms were full of excitement about making it a success. The business seminar they'd been to over the weekend had fired them up and they were ready to go.

"Kira, you need to go to work. Do you want to work with Harlow to the paper, at Big Pie Bakery, or down at Traveler?" Mom asked.

Kira flashed a deer-in-the-headlights look.

"Do I have to decide now?"

"Yes, you need to have a job. I promised your grandmother."

"Okay... well, can I try the paper first?"

Mom turned to me and raised her eyebrows.

"Yeah, that's okay," I said.

What else could I really do? Yes, the *Harlot Bay Reader* was absolutely failing and was barely a job, but I didn't really want to get into *that* at the family dinner. I decide to change the topic to the matter of Grandma April and the two real estate developers.

I told the moms about Dominic Gresso coming to the house over the weekend and wanting to buy the mansion and how he had investigators and had made some comments about Grandma not being seen for a long time. Then I told them about how Sylvester Coldwell had been in my office today, basically saying the same thing. By the time I was finished, the moms were looking a little worried, but not much. I had thought it would cause a full-blown panic.

"Well, you can distill a glamour again, can't you?" Aunt Ro said to Aunt Cass.

"Done and done," Aunt Cass said, taking another sip of wine.

"You guys have done this before?" Molly asked.

"Mom has been frozen for twenty years, so we've had to do a few things so no one got suspicious," Aunt Ro said.

"You're not interested in selling Torrent Mansion?" I asked.

"Goddess, no," Mom said. "Generations of Torrents of lived here and we're not going to be the ones who sell it. All those witches would probably return from the dead to haunt us if we ever did."

The rest of the dinner rolled on with everyone in fairly good spirits. I could see that Molly and Luce still wanted to say something to Aunt Cass about the pink hair dye and the nose piercing, but they held back because they didn't want Kira to get stressed again. Soon we finished dinner and then dessert, and it wasn't long before the four of us were back at our end of the mansion. Kira flopped down on the sofa and

Adams jumped into her lap and started kneading at her and purring.

"Your family is so different from mine," Kira said. "You can barely sneeze at my house without getting in trouble."

"That's what it's like here. I got in trouble once because I ate a piece of cheese," Adams said, starting to dribble now.

"You were in trouble for eating cheese when you opened the refrigerator, took the cheese out of the package and then ate most of it," I said.

"There is no justice for cats," Adams murmured. He was entering into his Zen mode where he'd be purring and dribbling all over whomever he was sitting on.

"You smell like lavender," Kira said.

Adams didn't respond but just kept purring. The four of us talked a bit before the various glasses of wine caught up with us and we all took ourselves off to bed. We left Kira sitting on the sofa with Adams, watching TV.

CHAPTER EIGHT

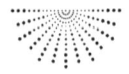

My beard was thick and itchy and I wanted to pull it off as soon as I put it on.

"Stop fiddling with it. It's going to fall off," Mom said, swiping my hand away.

"This costume is ridiculously hot," I complained.

The week had zipped by with uncommon haste. I'd gone to work a few times with Kira and gotten her to write a few little things for me before letting her go (she took herself off to the beach most days). There were no more fires and no more developments on that side of things. I hadn't heard from Detective Moreland and was starting to nurture a little hope that perhaps I was no longer a suspect. We had a few more family dinners, which generally went along as well as they normally did. Aunt Ro was especially touchy for some reason, but no one really knew why.

Now it was Sunday morning on a day that promised to be blistering, and I was dressed as Captain Blackbeard, wearing thick boots, heavy pants and an ornate brocade coat. I had a cutlass at my waist and fake pistols, a giant hat and a massive itchy beard.

We were gathered in the kitchen of Big Pie Bakery, getting ready. The moms were pretty much dressed in versions of my costume as well, with thick, heavy beards and cutlasses. Molly and Luce hadn't arrived yet, and their costumes was sitting on the countertop waiting for them.

"I hope she remembered to get enough fuel for the float," Aunt Ro worried. It was Molly's job to buy fuel. We'd hired one of the local teenagers to drive it after Kira had declined to participate in any way. The moms had still guilted her into turning up on the sidelines, though.

Oh, and in the last week I had written a letter to Jack, pretending I was an Incan princess ruling a dying empire. He'd written back to me pretending to be an astronaut heading to outer space. He'd also written that he expected to be back soon, but he wasn't quite sure when.

I finally managed to get my beard into a position where it wouldn't make me itchy. It was about ten in the morning and the parade was due to start soon. The route would take us all the way down the main street, left past the library and a bunch of other shops, left again past more shops and pretty much in a circle back to where we'd started before continuing down to Scarness Park, where it would become a free-for-all party. There would be tables selling food, people face painting, and an inflatable pirate ship, and we were expecting practically every tourist in the town plus everyone who lived here to be there. The mayor would open it with a speech (bets were being taken on the color of his hair).

With only fifteen minutes before the parade was due to start, Molly and Luce finally turned up.

"No way, if I have to wear this, you have to wear this," I said, pointing my cutlass at both of them.

They were pirates, technically. But they'd gone the sexy pirate route. Short skirts, thin shirts that could breathe and soft pirate hats.

"This is what female pirates wear," Molly said.

"Especially in this climate," Luce added.

I pointed my cutlass at the costumes sitting on top of the counter.

"Both of you put those on immediately or you're getting chopped," I said.

Luce and Molly were both wearing cutlasses as well. They pulled them out and we started sword fighting in the kitchen. I got a few good whacks in before the moms put a stop to it.

"It's too late now, let's go," Aunt Ro said, giving Molly a significant look.

We rushed out of the bakery and into the street. Not only was it sunny, but the humidity was quite high. I could feel my clothes sticking to me.

The streets were full of tourists and also people dressed up as pirates. There were at least fifty Blackbeards within sight. There were children wearing pirate hats and waving toy cutlasses running everywhere. We rushed down to where the parade floats were stored and found ours. The family had been working on it over the past week. Like many people, we'd gone the pirate ship route and had built the front half of a pirate ship with a giant mast on the top. There was a small car hidden beneath it. Our teenage driver, Michael, smiled with relief when we arrived.

"I thought you wouldn't be here," he said, his voice cracking a little.

I really feel sorry for teenagers sometimes. There you are, living your life, and then your entire body turns against you, giving you acne and making your voice break.

"We're here now and I am so glad to see you," Molly cooed to him.

Michael immediately turned bright red and then practically bolted away to climb through the small hidden door and into the car underneath the float.

"Leave the kid alone," I said to her.

"What? He's cute. I think it's adorable the way he blushes," Molly said, laughing.

Aunt Cass and Kira finally arrived. Kira had declined to dress up or participate in any way. She was going to watch from the sidelines and then come to Scarness Park to help out at the Big Pie Bakery table. Aunt Cass, on the other hand, had gone all the way. She was wearing an elaborate pirate costume with gigantic leather boots, flashy red pants and a coat that was covered in gold. She wore a gigantic fake beard, and when she pulled out a cutlass and waved around it looked very sharp and very deadly.

"Avast, ye landlubbers," Aunt Cass yelled at us as she walked up to the float.

"Is that… a real cutlass?" Molly asked.

"Arrrrr!" Aunt Cass said and slipped it back into its scabbard.

Inevitably the parade floats got started a little past when they should have because there were so many of them. There were at least five or six different pirate ships, a Truer Island, a gallows and quite a few rowboats. Blackbeard wasn't the only pirate represented. There were also a few Redbeards and people dressed as the other pirates who used to frequent this part of part of America. Not only that, there were some of the governors and soldiers who would help fight the pirates off. When we reached Scarness Park, the Governor would read out the charges against the pirates and there would be a mock battle.

Someone at the front of the parade blew a giant horn and the first float took off. It was just then that Will and Ollie came rushing up, dressed as pirates as well. They'd both gone with the bare-chested, wild hair, glinting gold jewelry, swashbuckling style of pirate. Molly and Luce kissed their boyfriends and then helped them up onto the float. The moms jumped up on the float as well and then I followed, helping Aunt Cass up. She stood on the prow, pulled out her shining cutlass and then yelled out "Anchors aweigh!"

Michael took off with such a jerk that we almost all fell down. We quickly regained our balance and then we were off. Down the main street, tourists lined both sides of the road. There weren't any barricades to stop them from walking in front of the floats, but thankfully most people had the sense not to step under them, and we were going so slowly that people could crisscross between the floats as we went. I pulled out my cutlass and scowled at the people on the sidewalk.

Aunt Cass was standing on the prow of our fake ship, in her element. I hadn't felt any magic, but I think she had done something to slightly magnify the sound of her voice, because every time she spoke, she seemed far louder than usual.

"Avast, ye landlubbers! Fear the wrath of Captain Blackbeard!" she boomed, pointing her cutlass at a group of children who burst into squeals and ran away giggling. We made it all the way down the main street until we hit the corner, where we came to a stop. One of the floats up ahead must've had a problem. I jumped off the front of the float and stood there for a little, waving my cutlass around. We got going after a minute or two.

As we turned the corner I saw there was another float up ahead on the side, waiting to join the parade. It was a giant ship. A gap opened up and the float pulled in ahead of us. Standing on its prow were two tall Blackbeards with shining cutlasses, waving them around.

They'd really gone all out on this float. They had an actual wooden mast with a long rope coiled around it.

One of the Blackbeards unwound the rope and leapt off the float. He swung out over the crowd and then landed directly in front of me. He pulled out his shining cutlass and stepped closer.

"Arrr, it's me, Captain Blackbeard, back from a long journey," he said, grinning.

He had a giant hat on and a thick beard obscuring his face, but those eyes, my gosh, those eyes that verged on blue and green were unmistakable.

It was Jack.

There had been letters going back and forth between us, and I'd imagined a hundred times when and how we'd see each other again. In some of my imaginings, he casually appeared at the mansion, standing at my front door with that smile of his. In others, I was walking on the beach and he walked out of the sea, water dripping off his body.

(C'mon, they're fantasies!)

I never would have imagined that he'd swing down dressed as Captain Blackbeard, swashbuckling with all his might.

"Arrr!" I said and then I wrapped my hands around him and kissed him as hard as I could.

It was a kiss a long time coming, a kiss that had been waiting impatiently, a kiss that could no longer be denied.

All around us the crowd went crazy cheering and laughing. When we pulled apart our beards stuck to each other for a moment.

"Wow," breathed Jack.

I had no words, so I grabbed his hand and lifted it in the air like we'd won a prize. The crowd around us cheered again and then Aunt Cass told us to get moving because we were holding up the parade.

I couldn't help smiling to myself as we walked along hand in hand. Life was good, and now it looked like it was about to get even better.

CHAPTER NINE

You know how they say that if a man asks you out on a date at the last minute, you're supposed to decline? Keep the mystery, you're too busy and so on?

The hell with that! I had a date!

I was waiting outside Valhalla Viking while Jack found somewhere to park his truck. With all the tourists flooding in, parking spots were at a premium. It was still pirate parade day and there were many Blackbeards roaming the streets (some drunk and looking more and more like real pirates as the festivities turned merry).

We'd walked hand in hand the rest of the parade until we had eventually reached the park. The mayor had given some crazy speech as usual and everyone cheered (he was dressed as a pirate, but imagine a pirate who'd been dipped in Technicolor paint). Jack and I'd found a quiet spot away from everyone else to grab a bite to eat and I'd discovered that the whole thing had been set up by the moms!

Jack had known he was coming back to town today. He'd arranged with them to participate in the pirate parade so he could come swashbuckling in. Jonas had built the float all by himself, including the wooden mast (he, of course, was the other Blackbeard).

I was amazed the whole thing had been set up just so Jack could come swinging in!

I had to admit I didn't mind this type of meddling. We had a thousand things to talk about, but then the moms had found us and pulled me over to the bakery table and put me to work. Jack had asked me out, and on the spot I said yes!

The moms were certainly beside themselves with glee at how successful their meddling had been. For the short time Jack was at the bakery table, Kira didn't say a single word. She only blushed and mumbled when he said hello. I could see why Molly kept teasing Michael. Teenagers can be quite adorable.

Sometimes.

And now, there I was waiting outside Valhalla Viking, watching tourists come and go, feeling on top of the world, when someone tapped me on the shoulder. I turned around with a smile, only to find Carter standing there. His arm was still in a sling and he was unshaven, which was unusual for him.

I felt my happiness falter, but then I recovered. Not even Carter could ruin my night!

"Hey, Carter, how you doing?" I said, the very essence of chirpiness.

"Not good. I fell through a broken step at my office and fractured my arm. When I told my real estate agent that they needed to repair the step, something I've been asking them to do for months, they responded by upping my rent and threatening to evict me. What do you know about Sylvester Coldwell?"

Wow, this was not good at all.

"Not much, I guess. He and his family own a lot of land

and control many properties in town. I don't like him very much, I can tell you that," I said.

"I started looking into his family's history. Do you know that his grandfather bought a few places that had burned to the ground and then developed them? That's how they got their start in Harlot Bay."

It was easy enough to see where he was going with this.

"I did know some of that. But there's not really any evidence, is there?" I asked.

"Behind every great fortune is a great crime," Carter said to me. He sighed and rubbed his stubble with his free hand. "Look... Coldwell squeezing me is going to cause serious problems for the *Harlot Bay Times*. I think there is something worth investigating regarding his family, and I want to ask you if you want to be involved because I know that you're good at that type of thing."

Yes, he said it while essentially looking at the sidewalk and mumbling through it, but it was still a compliment from Carter Wilkins. He wanted my help?

For a moment I felt a spiteful anger rising up... but then I let it go.

He looked so sad and defeated that I couldn't bring myself to smack him around despite what he had written about me and my family in the past.

"Okay, well... I guess I can help you. Do you want to trade background information or something like that?" I asked.

"I thought we could work on it together. I've been doing research and you have too, clearly. Let's put our heads together and then investigate more. How about I come to your office tomorrow? Maybe in the afternoon?"

"Yeah... that would be okay," I mumbled.

I was starting to realize that I would have to be around Carter if I was going to do any work with him. That didn't sound like something I would be interested in. It was too late, though – I'd agreed.

Carter smiled at me, again looking like a nervous dog, and walked away just as Jack approached, jingling his truck keys in his hand.

"At the Festival of Lights, you were sword fighting recorders with some guy. That was him, wasn't it?"

"That's the one. And… I just agreed to work with him for some reason. Maybe I have heatstroke from walking around in a pirate costume all day?"

Jack laughed, and just like that I didn't care whether I'd have to work with Carter.

We entered Valhalla Viking, which was packed with tourists. One of the waitresses, Carol, waved to me and then directed us to an empty booth near the back.

We sat down in the booth and Carol gave us our menus. She was dressed as a full Viking Shield Maiden with a golden breastplate, a horned silver helmet and her hair in braids.

Valhalla Viking is a themed restaurant and they take it seriously. They do serve beer, but you can also buy mead and it's served in imitation carved horns. There's a lot of meat on the menu and all the waiters and staff dress as Vikings. The inside of the bar and restaurant is dark and smoky. The tourists absolutely love it.

Carol zipped away, promising to return soon for our order.

"Would you like a beer?" Jack asked me.

"Absolutely," I said. While Jack went over to the bar, I browsed the menu, my stomach grumbling. There were so many delicious things I didn't know what to choose.

Jack soon returned with beers. We said cheers to the good health of all Vikings everywhere and then chose what we'd order. We finally settled on slow-cooked ribs to share, rough-cut potato wedges and something called Viking salad that didn't give many details but sounded interesting. Carol came to take our order and then there we were, sitting at the table, no one to interrupt us, *finally* together after such a long time apart.

Jack's hair was slightly longer and shaggy. He still had that rough stubble, and in the darkened restaurant I could see the glimmers of the small lights around us reflected in his eyes.

Upon hearing that I was going to go on a date with Jack, Molly and Luce had taken it upon themselves to dress me. There had been somewhat of a battle between the "low-cut, short skirt" side of things and the "slightly more demure but still a bit sexy" side. I think if Molly had had her way I would have turned up to this dinner in a push-up bra and panties! I'd finally settled on a blue dress that was still a little demure. Between a good dress, small golden earrings, makeup and red lipstick, I was, for once, not feeling like a poor small-town country girl. That was mostly thanks to Mom handing me some cash and telling me to have a good time.

"So," Jack said, smiling at me.

"So," I whispered.

"That was some kiss. Do you think that's how Blackbeard actually kissed?"

I felt myself blush but in the darkness, he couldn't see it. Yes, I'd kissed him. Then shortly after that, shyness had come rushing back.

"Blackbeard was a great kisser. That's a historical fact," I said.

"Historical fact? That's amazing," Jack said, laughing. He threw his head back as he did in a laugh that shook his whole body. Some quiet voice inside me whispered *this is the one*.

The dinner raced by with unfair speed. The meal was extraordinary. The meat was falling off the ribs. It was perfectly paired with a smoky sauce. The rough-cut wedges were salty and delicious, and the Viking salad turned about out to be a crazy mixture that I'm sure no Viking ever actually ate. It was hard to tell in the darkness, but I'm sure it had flower petals in it. We ordered more beer, which offset the salty wedges, and talked about anything and everything. Jack told me he'd taken so long to return because he had to sell his house and getting all that in order was a difficult task. He'd had to arrange repairs and maintenance and painting. Like all projects, even if you assumed it would take a long time, it always took twice as long as you thought.

I didn't have much to tell him about Harlot Bay. Not very much had happened while he'd been gone. The ice-skating rink renovations were slowly starting. The council was still debating what to do about the burned-out lighthouse. Traveler was well on its way to becoming a thriving coffee shop, and the Torrent Mansion Bed-and-Breakfast was now up and running. The conversation flowed all over the place and it was simply wonderful. I found myself laughing again and again, feeling so happy I thought my heart would burst.

Soon we finished our meal and both of us were too full to have any dessert. We left Valhalla and Jack suggested we go for a walk, maybe to the point that overlooked the ocean.

I started laughing the moment he suggested it.

"What? You don't want to go up to the point?"

"You want to go to Make-Out Point?" I said, gasping for air.

"Is *that* what the kids call it?" Jack said, understanding.

"No, it's fine, we can go to Make-Out Point. Teenagers *love* it. It's awesome up there," I said, still giggling to myself.

"Okay, well, I'm not from around here, cheeky chops. What if we walk on the beach instead?"

"Romantic Stroll on the Moonlight Beach? You want to go to that one?" I said, poking him in the ribs.

I was still laughing as we headed off down the street,

joining the streams of tourists all around us. Waiting on the corner for a car to pass, I caught a flash of pink hair and a glint of silver down a side street. I glanced and saw a teenager, but in the dark I couldn't be sure if it was Kira or not. It certainly looked like her. Not that I was keeping track, but I'd thought she was at home tonight.

"See someone you know?" Jack asked.

"I think it was Kira. The teenage girl who's staying with us at the moment. I don't know," I said.

"Is she not allowed out at night?"

"No, I don't think she usually is. Her grandmother is fairly strict, but she is living with us at the moment and we don't have the same rules, most of the time."

"Why is she living with you?" Jack asked.

Eeep.

I'd blundered into a topic that I couldn't give a straight answer to. What could I say? *Well, she's a Slip Witch and she's being trained by my great-aunt who is also a Slip Witch. Oh, by the way, Grandma is in the basement and she's been frozen in time for the last twenty years.*

My lying skills kicked into gear.

"Kira has been having trouble at school. My aunt and Kira's grandma are friends and thought a change of scenery might help."

Okay, not that bad of a lie.

"We had a friend who did that. He lived with us for a while growing up because things weren't so good back home. It's a good thing to do," Jack said.

We walked on and soon were down on the beach. I took off my shoes. The sand was still warm from the sun of the day. Soon we were barefoot, walking along by the water's edge, not talking about much in particular. The moon was sailing high above Harlot Bay, lighting up the entire beach, and we kept passing couples walking hand in hand, giggling and talking. We hadn't walked far when some nothing joke between us had us laughing and teasing each other, and soon the distance between us vanished and we kissed again. I could almost feel myself floating off the ground with Jack's strong arms wrapped around me.

It was then, in the midst of a kiss that I never wanted to end, that I felt something clench inside me like a hot coal had been dropped in my stomach. It was like a fishhook, pulling at me, leading up somewhere into the hills that overlooked Harlot Bay.

I broke apart from Jack and gasped.

"Are you okay?"

The pain in my stomach spiked and there was a pull towards the hills. I looked up into the darkness to see the first flickers of orange flame. There was a fire.

"I'm okay. Saw *that* out of the corner of my eye. It gave me a shock," I said, pointing at the small glow.

"Is that a fire?" Jack asked.

"Could be the arsonist," I said.

We'd spoken briefly during dinner about some of the fires in Harlot Bay. We'd quickly moved on from that sad topic to something far more fun.

The hot coal in my stomach pulled again. I had to get closer to the fire.

"Let's go and check it out," I said.

"Okay," Jack replied.

We jogged back up the beach. With every step towards the fire, the pain in my stomach lessened. Soon we were back up on the Esplanade, putting our shoes on.

"I'm parked over here. I had to park so far away because there wasn't anywhere near the restaurant," Jack said.

We rushed over to his truck and jumped in. We'd had a few beers during dinner, but not so many it wasn't safe to drive.

Jack's truck smelled like man and wood shavings and aged leather. On any other occasion, I would have loved sitting there next to him, driving through the darkness of Harlot Bay, but now all I could feel was anxiety. The hot coal in my stomach was a tugging pain, urging me to come closer to the fire.

We raced up out of Harlot Bay as fast as we could, which wasn't really that fast because of all the tourists crossing the streets. We finally got out of the main part of the town and made our way up into the hills. The small flickering glow of fire was growing larger by the second. And as we raced along I heard the wail of the fire siren.

We reached the fire at the same time as the fire engine and got out of the truck. In front of us was a beautiful old wooden two-story house painted in bright colors with gigantic windows that looked out over the sea in one direction and the town in the other. They had a large green hedge surrounding most of the property. The fire had started there. The hedge was burning, flinging embers up into the sky, crackling and popping as the sap caught fire.

We watched as the firefighters set up their hoses and started trying to contain the blaze. There was a couple standing out on the road, a man and a woman. She was crying and he was trying to comfort her, but he looked worried too. They were probably the owners. All along the street, neighbors were slowly emerging from their homes to watch the firefighters. Now that I was standing twenty feet away, the hot coal feeling and the pull had disappeared. I looked around, hoping to see anyone who might have been at the last fire. Perhaps I could catch the arsonist (if in fact there was one). I had no idea what a fire spirit looked like or if it would even be visible to me or anyone else.

The firefighters soon got the blaze under control and I didn't see anyone I recognized.

That was until the arson investigator, Detective Moreland, arrived in his shiny black car. I quickly got back in the truck and asked Jack to take me home. We drove away, but I'm fairly sure the investigator saw me.

It really seemed our romantic night was at an end. The fire had taken away all of our laughing and joking. Both of us were on edge. Jack drove me home and walked me up to the front door.

I was feeling anxious and unsure, butterflies fluttering in my stomach, worrying that soon I'd see Detective Moreland again. I had no idea why I'd felt drawn to the fire. What if it happened again?

At the front door, I turned around and looked into Jack's eyes and then all my worries disappeared for a moment.

"Let's do this again sometime... except without the fire. I'm out of town for a few days. Let's have lunch when I'm back," Jack said. Then we kissed. I could smell his aftershave, the tinge of smoke from the hedge fire, the faint scent of wood shavings. The kiss was interrupted by the sound of my cousins inside the house calling out *woooooo* through the front door. We broke apart, both of us grinning. I agreed to lunch, we said good night and then I went inside. Molly and Luce pounced on me like lionesses out on the hunt.

"You kissed him. Are you going to have his babies now?" Luce asked.

"Do you have their names picked out?" Molly added.

"Shut up," I said, laughing. I was happy, too giddy to care much about anything.

Molly and Luce demanded a complete debrief of every moment from when he picked me up at home, all the way to Valhalla Viking, our dinner, the beach and anything else. They were sighing and oohing the whole time until I told them about the sudden feeling of a hot coal appearing in my stomach and the pull of the fishhook dragging me to the fire.

Their faces went very solemn.

"Do you think it's you starting the fires?" Molly said, as gently as possible.

"It's not me. It feels completely different from when I do it," I said.

"If it's not you, why would you be pulled to the fire?" Luce asked.

I shrugged and gave the same answer I've given many, many times in my life.

"I'm a Slip Witch. It sucks," I said.

I told them we'd left when the fire had been extinguished, but not before Detective Moreland had arrived. Molly and Luce didn't like the sound of that at all.

I wanted to get off the topic as quickly as possible, so I told them how I'd stupidly agreed to work with Carter on investigating Sylvester Coldwell and his family.

"Carter seems to think that he might be behind some of these fires. He researched Coldwell's grandfather and discovered that's how they got their start being rich," I said.

"Speaking of rich, do you remember Richie Coldwell from school? Goddess, that guy was an arrogant little dishrag," Molly said.

"Wasn't he the one that kept trying to get us to come around to see his so-called awesome hot tub?" Luce asked.

"Yeah. That was all he did, try to get people to come around to his dad's house to show off how rich he was. So glad he left town," Molly said.

"So do you really think that Sylvester could be behind some of the fires?" Luce asked.

"I don't know. I don't like him. He's a sleazy little toad, but then Aunt Cass said it was a fire spirit. We even set up beacons to catch it."

I'd forgotten the beacons up until now! If the fire tonight was the fire spirit, perhaps Aunt Cass knew where it was now. Right on cue, my phone rang, coming from an unlisted number. "Hello?"

It was Aunt Cass.

"You and Kira need to collect the beacons in the morning and bring them here," Aunt Cass said.

"When did you get a phone?" I asked.

"None of your business. Are you going to get them in the morning or not?"

"Okay, okay," I said before Aunt Cass hung up on me.

"Sheesh, she's in a mood. I have to collect the beacons in the morning with Kira. So it looks like it was a fire spirit," I told Molly and Luce.

"I don't like the idea of fire spirits burning things down," Luce said. "But then, what if it's like a baby or something? He could be scared or lost."

I saw Molly rolling her eyes behind Luce. No matter what evil thing existed in the world, Luce was always sure it had a good side. She especially cared about small animals, even if they could kill you.

I went to bed after wiping off my makeup and taking out my earrings. I could still smell the faint scent of Jack where he had touched me. His cologne was on my hands. As Adams settled in at the foot of my bed, again smelling like lavender quite strongly, I drifted to sleep with the faint scent of Jack helping me float away.

CHAPTER TEN

*K*ira was one grumpy sleep-deprived teenager who barely said a word to me until we reached the lighthouse. It was seven in the morning and I'd been awakened by Aunt Cass demanding I get out to recover the beacons as soon as possible. I hadn't even had time to shower, so I'd made some toast and gulped down a coffee as fast as I could while a very tired Kira did the same.

At the lighthouse, it was still quite cool this early and there were no tourists around.

"Can you unlock it?" I asked Kira. She grunted something at me, but then cast an unlocking spell. We made our way inside and found that someone had been cleaning during the week. It appeared they'd been using a pressure washer against the walls to remove the soot from the fire. There was a pile of new lumber and other bits and pieces over against one wall. Was someone restoring the lighthouse?

"I guess I have to float the beacon down too?" Kira said to me with about as much snark as anyone could possibly have at this time of day.

"If you want to," I said. Kira didn't answer again. She cast a levitation spell and managed to lift the beacon off the high windowsill and float it down. Although she was still very much in her silent sarcastic teenager mode, I could see she was very happy at having cast a spell and lowered the beacon without any problem.

"Cool," Kira said, catching the beacon in her hand. It had a crystal in the middle of it that had been pure white. Now it was tinted with orange, like tiny sparks of fire. Kira carefully put it in her pocket and then gave me an apologetic smile.

"Sorry, didn't sleep very well last night," she said.

I remembered that I'd seen a girl with pink hair and a silver piercing last night in Harlot Bay. I also realized that Kira hadn't been down on our end of the mansion when I'd come home. I guess I'd assumed that she was already in bed, asleep.

What did I do with these realizations? Did I relax about it and not ask Kira questions about where she was last night and hope that eventually she would trust me enough to talk openly? Or did I blunder in like an idiot?

Ding ding! If you chose blundering like an idiot, you win a hundred dollars!

"Did I see you last night in Harlot Bay? What were you doing out?"

The look Kira gave me could have frozen the sun into a block of ice.

"Let's get the other ones," she said.

"It's okay if you were out. I'm just asking. In fact, I know you were out because when I came home you weren't there."

Yep, that's right. Compounding error upon error.

"I went to bed early and I was asleep. I guess you just didn't bother to check on me," Kira said.

I knew teenage obstinacy well. My cousins and I'd been exactly the same way. Doing that dumb thing where you tell lies even in the face of overwhelming evidence. Rather than push it, I let it go.

We recovered the second beacon as easily as the first and then we were at the creepy murder house. Kira hadn't spoken a word to me since the lighthouse. That was fine with me. I had bigger things on my mind than a teenager being upset at me.

We rushed in, recovered the beacon and rushed back out. We returned to the mansion and Kira sullenly followed me inside. Aunt Cass was waiting for us. Kira handed over the three beacons.

"Excellent, this is perfect," Aunt Cass said, examining one critically. It was even darker than the first we'd recovered, appearing to have small flames embedded in the crystal.

"You can track down the fire spirit now?" I asked.

"Maybe. You two can go now. I need to study these," Aunt Cass said, dismissing us with a wave of the hand. She walked away, heading for the kitchen, obviously going to her underground investigation room.

"Wait, I need to talk about something that happened last night!" I said.

Aunt Cass gave a dramatic sigh and then turned around and came walking back.

"Well, what is it?"

"It was last night, when I was on the beach with Jack," I began. I told her as quickly as possible about the feeling of the hot coal and the pull that led me to the fire.

"The very short answer is you're a Slip Witch. The fire spirit is a magical entity. You probably felt the pull because you were nearby."

"Do you think that's going to happen again?"

"It might. Could be useful in tracking the fire spirit. Don't be so worried about it."

"I'm not worried about it!" I said, at a much higher

volume than I intended. I heard Kira make some sort of dismissive snorting noise behind me, but before I could say anything to her, she walked out the front door.

"I need to look at this right now. Take Kira to work with you today," Aunt Cass said.

I groaned.

"It was fine last week, but now she's being so... annoying," I said.

"Yes, teenagers can be annoying," Aunt Cass replied evenly. I could feel the tone in her voice and hear the unspoken sentence: *just like you were.*

"Okay, okay, I get your point. Please hurry up and find the fire spirit, because I don't want to get pulled to another fire and I definitely don't want that detective seeing me at one. Okay?"

"Fine," Aunt Cass said and marched off through the kitchen.

I sighed a sigh that covered cranky great-aunts and frustratingly annoying teenagers. I'd take Kira to work with me, but what I was intending to do was send her to the beach as soon as possible. That plan disappeared when Aunt Cass pushed the kitchen door open.

"No letting her go to the beach. She has to stay with you," Aunt Cass said and then vanished before I could retort.

Feeling like this day was going to suck in about six different ways, I trudged my way back to our end of the house and got myself ready for a day of suckage.

CHAPTER ELEVEN

We were ending hour two of the silent treatment when John walked through the closed door. Kira was slumped on the sofa tapping away on her phone. She gasped in shock and dropped it.

"Oh, sorry, didn't mean to scare you," John said.

Kira quickly recovered, grabbing her phone and diving back into it.

"I wasn't scared," she said, tapping away furiously.

"You can see ghosts?" I asked.

"Ah, yeah," Kira said at maximum sarcasm.

"You look familiar to me. Do I know your mother?"

"I don't know."

"Her grandmother is Hattie Stern," I said.

"Hmm... nope, doesn't ring a bell."

A while ago, John had seen Hattie Stern walking past the office and had suddenly remembered he disliked her intensely. He'd called her an interfering busybody but had very quickly forgotten this and thus far hadn't remembered it again.

John sat down beside Kira and looked with interest at the

phone in her hand. Although he'd seen mine plenty of times, it seemed this particular piece of technology didn't stick in his mind. He was always fascinated by them.

"What is that?" John asked.

Kira looked at me and gave a dramatic sigh.

"Can I go to the beach now?"

"Nope. Sit over here while I do the counseling session," I said.

We swapped positions, Kira taking my place at the desk. Today I was asking more historical questions about Harlot Bay. Sometimes John gave interesting answers that indicated he had most likely been living in Harlot Bay when he died. I'd planned to talk about the old businesses, but then I remembered all the fires that I'd researched, so I started with that instead.

"A long time ago a skating rink burned down. Do you remember?"

"Oh yes, I remember that. The fire burned for two days before they could put it out. When they scraped the ashes away, they built shops there."

"Do you remember if they thought someone had started it deliberately?"

"Started what?"

"The fire."

"What fire are you talking about? The one at the house?"

Kira gave another exasperated sigh from her chair. I shot her a glance to tell her to shut up but honestly, it was easy to get frustrated with John's memory problems. He could literally forget what he was talking about between one sentence and the next.

We carried on the counseling session over the next hour but like pretty much every other session we'd ever had, we didn't really get anywhere.

Soon we were done. John pulled a twenty-dollar bill from

somewhere (still wasn't sure where they came from) and left it on the table. He said goodbye to Kira, who merely grunted in return.

"So, this is like your job or whatever?" Kira asked as soon as he was gone.

She was being intensely sarcastic again and after hearing her being rude to John, I was in no mood to take it. I grabbed the arms of her chair and pulled her towards me. I was getting angry but I didn't want to yell at her.

I took her hands between mine and looked directly into her eyes.

"Kira, I know you're angry at me about what I said this morning. I'm sorry about that. I shouldn't have said that. But enough is enough. You cannot spend hours sulking and giving people the silent treatment. You cannot be rude and mean to people, even dead ones. You're stuck with us for who knows how long, so how about you make it nice and easy for all of us?" I said.

Kira bit her lip and then frowned before looking away. I was still holding a hand when I felt the jolt of magic. She Slipped. Hazy lines of color appeared around us, like auras stretched out into string. There was a blue line running across the floor, and a green one with pink stripes sliding out the window. A deep red string seemed to emerge from my stomach and run out through the door and down the stairs.

"Not again," Kira whispered.

"What is this?"

"I don't know. Sometimes the strings go places where bad stuff happens. Like that one there," Kira said, pointing at the deep red string that was coming from me. I let go of her hand, but the strings didn't disappear. Maybe I could see it if I stayed close to Kira.

"Do you mean something bad is going to happen to me?"

"I don't know, but it probably leads somewhere bad. I think that one is a fire," she said.

I could see she was almost on the verge of tears. I stood up and pulled Kira up out of the chair and gave her quick hug. She stiffened at first but then relaxed, clasping her hands behind my back.

"It's okay. The best thing to do with Slip magic is confront it. We'll follow the line and see where it goes."

"Okay," Kira said in a muffled whisper. We locked up the office and went outside. The deep red string stretched off down the street and around the corner. It was strange it didn't go *through* buildings but rather went the way a person would out on the sidewalk or road. Outside, I noticed Kira had a red line attached to her as well that was tangled up with the deep red one. There were other lines on the street running in all directions including a vibrant yellow one that seemed almost cheerful.

"What's that one?" I asked.

"Probably my grandmother," Kira said.

"Seriously? I get happy feelings from it," I said.

"She probably got a neighbor in trouble for leaving their trash can out for an extra day or something like that. She'd be happy about that," Kira said and then gave me a little smile.

We got into my car and after a few false starts finally got going. The streets were still packed with tourists who were oblivious to the magic lines running through them. We followed the red line down the street and around the corner and to the edge of town, where it entered a lot of empty warehouses.

It was surrounded by a fence and a locked gate, but that wasn't going to stop two Slip Witches. We got out of the car, and a moment later the gate was open.

Making sure no one was around, we followed the red line

past stacked pallets and a row of dumpsters until we finally came to a warehouse with a locked door. This one was barred from the inside, so we walked around until we found a window we could open.

"Isn't this illegal?" Kira asked as I prepared to lift her through the window.

"I'm a journalist and you're my assistant. It's not illegal, it's newsgathering," I said. "Now get inside before someone sees us."

I help Kira through the window, and then after a few minutes she found some boxes to stand on. She reached back to pull me up and in.

Inside the warehouse was mostly empty. There were pallets lying about the place and some drums in the back corner. The red line went up some stairs and finally terminated in an old abandoned office, stopping in the middle of the floor.

"Well, this is a big bust," Kira said, poking around the office. She looked through an old filing cabinet while I searched the desk drawers. All I found was a very faded receipt for some car repairs. The filing cabinet was empty.

We left the office and spent maybe ten minutes walking around the entire warehouse, looking for anything that would give a clue as to why the red line was there, but we didn't find anything. The place was unused and certainly didn't look to be a candidate to be burnt down anytime soon (apart from it being an empty warehouse). We did discover that if I was more than ten feet away from Kira, the lines vanished for me. It was definitely her Slip Witch power, not mine.

Our investigation at a dead end, we drove back to my office and went upstairs. Kira slumped down on the sofa, obviously bored, and I sat at the desk. We talked about what the lines might mean but didn't come up with anything new.

In fact, a few minutes after we returned, the lines vanished entirely.

"Will they come back?" I asked.

"They probably will. It usually seems to go for a few days at a time," Kira said.

I was searching the Internet to discover who owned that warehouse when Kira gave another dramatic sigh and then stood up from the sofa.

"Being a journalist and breaking and entering is awesome and fun, but this is *sooooo* boring. I might go to work at the bakery instead."

"Yeah, it's not as exciting as people think," I said.

"See you later," Kira said.

She was gone in a flash. She'd obviously learned the lesson that most children and teenagers grasp quickly: as soon as an adult agrees to let you do something, get out of there before they can change their mind.

The rest of the morning passed quickly. I found the owners of the warehouse, but it didn't really tell me anything special. Soon it was lunch and I wandered out over to Traveler. Molly and Luce were behind the counter today and both shook their heads at me as I waved through the window.

Over the last week some of the renovations had been done at night and now there were chairs and tables built in that were filled with chatting tourists. The big renovation, which was taking the entire cash register counter area and moving the whole thing back to allow more space, would be coming in a few days. They'd have to shut down the shop for that.

I ended up having lunch alone, once again wishing Jack and I'd actually traded phone numbers, which for some reason we hadn't.

Despite the fact that the *Harlot Bay Reader* was going very badly, I could feel the excitement of the journalistic chase inside me.

Carter was possibly on to something with the history of fires in town. Aunt Cass was tracking a fire spirit. There would be a break in this case any day now.

I spent the rest the day researching the Coldwell real estate agency and family, digging into their background and pulling up anything I could find. It was true that they'd bought some of the sites that had burnt down, but so had other real estate agencies, including Dominic Gresso's (presumably his father) and some others. It seemed people didn't particularly want to buy land where the previous house or business had burnt down. The real estate agents would buy and develop them.

Carter had said last night he'd see me today but he didn't turn up. I wasn't too upset about it. The idea of working with him was not the biggest thrill of my life.

The end of the day came soon enough and soon I was at home. My cousins were still at work, so I went up to the main part of the mansion to find Mom and Kira in the kitchen making a cake together. It was a rare scene of domestic bliss.

I disrupted this scene of domestic bliss approximately one second later when I completely stuck my foot in it.

"How was the bakery today?" I asked Kira. Mom spun so fast she was a blur.

"Did you come to the bakery today?" she asked Kira.

"Um…"

Oh crap. Okay, so Kira had lied to me and hadn't gone to work at the bakery, and then I'd asked a question that had led to her getting caught. I had to think quick.

"I sent her to get me a donut. She must've gone to Green Palace instead."

"Ah, yeah. They were okay. Not as good as Big Pie," Kira said.

I was mentally urging her to keep her mouth shut and not elaborate on any details.

Mom fixed her gaze on me, but I was cool as a cucumber on an iceberg. I didn't crack, and after a moment she gave up.

"They use artificial sweeteners, you know," she muttered before turning back to the cake mixture. I gave Kira a subtle sign to get out of the kitchen as fast as possible. She did this by pulling out her phone and exclaiming that someone had tried to call her. She vanished into the dining room.

I was half a step behind her when Mom called out to me.

"She's supposed to be at work with you, not at the beach," Mom said.

"She was at work with me," I protested.

"Hmm…"

I kept my mouth shut, waiting for the slight sniff from Mom to indicate that the conversation was over, but then she changed topics.

"Do you know what's going on with Ro?"

"No. I mean, she seems a little extra crabby this week, but it can happen to anyone," I said.

"She's a little more than extra crabby. I thought maybe there was something else going on that we didn't know about. You know she hasn't been going to yoga this week?"

"I hadn't noticed," I said, not really sure where this was going.

"She is your family and she's not happy right now. Maybe you could find out why."

She started mixing the cake batter with an expression on her face that clearly said that this conversation was over. I didn't really want to get into anything further, so I simply said I would look into it and then got out of there.

When I returned to our end of the house, Kira was sitting on the sofa and Molly and Luce had just arrived home.

"Thanks for covering for me," Kira said. Molly and Luce's ears perked up at this.

"Covering for what?" Molly asked.

"Do you have a secret boyfriend?" Luce teased.

"Ignore them. You really gotta learn to lie better if you want to get away with things. *Never* give a specific location," I said.

"Yeah, say you're going out for a walk or something like that," Molly said.

"If you're staying at someone's house, say it's only you and no one else, then they can't check with any other parents," Luce added.

"If planning on seeing a boy –" Molly started to say.

"*That's* enough criminal tips right now," I interrupted, cutting Molly off.

I saw Molly wink at Kira and she mouthed *talk later.*

"Mom thinks you went to the beach today, but she is going to pretend that the lie we told was the truth," I said.

"Even though she knows it's not?" Kira asked.

"Sometimes it's easy to accept a little white lie in the interests of peace."

"That should really be our family motto," Molly said.

CHAPTER TWELVE

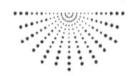

After a restless night where I dreamed of red lines stretching down the street and for some reason, Carter Wilkins, I was up early eating breakfast with Kira, Molly and Luce when a shiny black car parked in front of the mansion.

It was Sheriff Hardy and the arson investigator, Detective Moreland.

Sheriff Hardy's face was grave and grim. This was no social call. We all came to the front door.

"Sheriff Hardy, how can we help you?" I asked.

Detective Moreland had his notepad out again and apparently was writing down everything that I said. He scribbled something and then looked back at me with his blank face.

"Harlow, you and another girl, I believe called Kira, were seen at the warehouses on Torquay Road. They burnt down last night. We need you to come to the police station for questioning."

My breakfast churned in my stomach. Behind me, Kira made a squeaking sound.

I saw Aunt Cass rushing down from the mansion. She

was dressed in her standard harmless-little-old-lady clothes but wearing the thick pirate boots. She still had the pink streak in her hair, and the silver nose piercing caught the early morning sun.

"Are they under arrest?" Aunt Cass demanded.

"No, but we would like them to come to the station to answer some questions," Sheriff Hardy said.

Aunt Cass looked Detective Moreland up and down as though she was peering into his very soul.

"How about we do the questioning right here and right now?"

Detective Moreland apparently wrote this down in his notepad before turning to Aunt Cass.

"They're not under arrest, although we could very easily arrest them. I'd prefer not to have to arrest a member of Harlot Bay's media and the teenage girl your family is looking after. So please come to the police station for questioning. You can come if you want."

Aunt Cass seemed to consider this for a moment before she nodded.

"Okay, fine, but if I don't like your questions, we're out of there."

Kira stayed home with Molly and Luce, who told us they would take her into work today. There was no way Aunt Cass was going to let Kira be questioned. Anything could go wrong, including nearby paperwork bursting into flames.

The sheriff drove us to the police station in the back of the police car, so Aunt Cass and I didn't get a chance to clarify *what* exactly we were going to do. I was frantically racking my brains for a legitimate excuse as to why we had broken into an abandoned warehouse that then later burnt down. What clue would possibly lead me there?

The only thing that was even vaguely close was that I'd been researching the history of fires in Harlot Bay and had concluded that it was usually some abandoned business location that burned down. It was an incredible coincidence that I'd gone to one on a hunch.

It was weak, even I could see that, but it was the best I had at the moment. If I could convince Detective Moreland that I was just a journalist in the wrong spot at the wrong time, then perhaps it would be okay. Although I didn't really have any excuse for why I was at the hedge fire except for I was close and happened to see it from the beach. I wasn't really sure how long my "I'm a journalist" excuse would hold up.

We went into the police station and ended up in one of the rooms used for questioning suspects.

Sheriff Hardy gave me an apologetic look as Aunt Cass and I took our seats. It seemed his hands were tied. Being in the interrogation room made that ball of anxiety start in my stomach again. The chairs were cold steel, and there was a single steel table attached to the ground. There was a slot through it used to loop handcuffs to hold suspects so they couldn't escape or attack anyone. We hadn't been handcuffed, but still it was chilling.

Sheriff Hardy did retrieve some plastic cups for water and left a plastic jug on the table for us. I saw Detective Moreland give him a long hard look when he brought them, in but Sheriff Hardy ignored him.

Detective Moreland sat down, pulled out a clipboard and ran his finger down it.

"Quite a history of fires in Harlot Bay, isn't there? You've lived here most of your life?"

Of my many skills, reading upside-down is one of the least usable. Right now, though, it was perfect. I read down the list of fires and dates on his clipboard that stretched back over fifty years.

"You mean to ask me if I was out starting fires when I was three years old? You think I'm good for the old mill burning down? Yeah, you're right, you got me. I toddled out there and burned it to the ground. Well done."

I don't know where the sarcasm came from, possibly from spending too much time with a teenager, but it certainly helped push the anxiety away.

"Harlow," Sheriff Hardy murmured.

"Of course you didn't burn the old mill down, you were only three years old. That would mean that someone else did it, possibly from a family of arsonists," Detective Moreland said. He looked back at his clipboard.

"For example, I see that last year the apartment complex where you were living burnt down after some faulty wiring caught fire. I then further see that when you returned to Harlot Bay to live with your family in a house on the property, it subsequently burned down only three days later."

"That was bad wiring," Aunt Cass said, a chill in her voice.

"Yes, I understand there is a lot of bad wiring around Harlow. I guess there must've been some bad wiring at Zero Bend's vacation rental as well."

"Everyone knows he was being drugged by his diabolical manager. The cause of the fire was determined to be a kettle left on the stove top," I said.

"That's three fires where you were on the scene before they occurred. Most people have zero fires in their lives. Those who have *one* rarely have another. You can see how it appears suspicious, can't you?"

"The bad wiring was confirmed by investigation, both at the apartments and then at our property. I was at Zero Bend's because I'm a journalist and sometimes when you're investigating crazy and/or drugged people, things happen."

I was now thinking that us saying yes to being questioned was about the dumbest thing we'd done in the history of time. All I could hope was that if I said something truly stupid that made it seem like we were suspects in all the fires,

Aunt Cass had some magic she could use to wipe out the recording and blank out memories. I had no idea whether this would be possible, of course.

"What were you doing yesterday at the warehouse on Torquay Road?" Detective Moreland asked.

Here it was, time to try out my pathetic lie.

"I've been researching the fires occurring in Harlot Bay. Myself and another journalist, Carter Wilkins, think that there is an arsonist who has been burning down buildings so they can possibly buy the empty land for development. We've been looking at Coldwell Associates, a local real estate agency. Yesterday I had been researching the nature of these fires and had concluded that they often occur in abandoned buildings. Knowing that the warehouses on the side of town fit this profile, I decided to go over there to see if I could find anything."

"So it was a hunch? Or intuition?"

"You could call it that. It was obviously a very bad coincidence for me, given that I went in there, didn't find anything, and then the warehouse burnt down."

"You realize it's illegal to break and enter buildings?" Detective Moreland said.

"I was investigating a story, trying to get to the bottom of it. Plenty of things are illegal when you're a reporter, but we still do it."

"Do you find it *incredibly* coincidental that the place you investigated happened to burn down?"

"I don't know what to say. I think it proves my hunch was right – the arsonist is targeting abandoned buildings. Perhaps you should look into that."

Detective Moreland nodded, wrote something down on his piece of paper and then flipped it over to a new sheet of questions. Although it seemed to take forever, in the end the interview was about an hour. Aunt Cass actually stayed silent for most of it. Detective Moreland went back through all these questions again, getting me to repeat the same stories, obviously searching for any detail that was out of place.

I was once again reminded that you should never ever talk to the police and never say yes to an interview under any circumstances. The best course was to keep your mouth shut until you could speak with a lawyer. That's how they get you. The urge to explain, to protest your innocence, to tell your side of the story. They're so good at it. Just trying to make it as though it is just a friendly chat when in fact they're gathering what may send you to jail. Soon enough, the interview was over and we were out of there.

CHAPTER THIRTEEN

On the way home in a taxi, Aunt Cass was uncharacteristically quiet. Normally she would have plenty to say about the police force.

"Have you found anything that could possibly clear us?" I asked.

"Something went wrong with the beacons," she muttered, chewing her bottom lip. She waved her hand at the driver and blocked him from hearing us.

"What do you mean? Did you *not* find what or who started the hedge fire?"

"I think there could be more than one fire spirit. There were multiple locations and it was all distorted by something. I'm going to need to put up more beacons around town."

"Do you need me and Kira to do that?"

"No, I'll do it."

I had the opportunity to tell Aunt Cass about Kira slipping yesterday and the red line we had seen. I knew I could trust her, in the sense that she wouldn't tell the moms, but I couldn't break Kira's trust. Teenagers will only trust you if you are one hundred percent trustworthy. If I revealed the Slip magic to Aunt Cass and then Kira found out, that could destroy our relationship. The only thing I could do would be to encourage Kira to tell Aunt Cass herself. Despite knowing it might help, I kept my mouth shut.

Besides, there were bigger fish to fry. Soon the moms would find out that we'd been taken in for questioning, and then I was sure the proverbial donut would hit the fan.

At home, Aunt Cass stomped inside without another word. I zipped to my car and went to work. I'd been there an hour when Mom called.

"You okay?" she asked.

I was expecting her to give me the third degree, so this took me by surprise.

"I guess so. It's not nice knowing they think I'm a suspect."

"What were you and Kira doing at that warehouse yesterday?"

I knew Mom wouldn't accept the "doing background research" lie, but again I couldn't give away Kira's private information. So I lied.

"I Slipped yesterday and saw a glowing line, like an aura that had been stretched out. I followed and it led there."

"It might be the arsonist, Harlow. If you find another one of them, you need to find some way to tell Sheriff Hardy, okay?"

"I'll try," I said, giving the ultimate in non-yes agreement.

"See that you do," Mom said and hung up.

Despite the fact I had a lunch date set up with Jack tomorrow and I knew he was out of town, I still wished he was around. Why couldn't the lunch date be today? I really needed it. Besides that, I couldn't help thinking of those eyes and that stubble and kissing him again.

I returned to the world of researching arson, digging into

everything I could. I took a quick break for lunch, zipping out to grab a sandwich and then coming back again to spend the rest of the afternoon gathering as much information as I could.

There was still no clear thread to it all. Housing and businesses burned down. Sometimes they were bought by developers after the fire. There was no big red glaring arrow pointing to a crime. It was though I had all the pieces of the jigsaw but I couldn't fit it together. Even if I could piece it all together, it was just as likely it would say *coincidence* in big fiery letters.

In the middle of the afternoon, Adams stepped out of nowhere, jumped up on my sofa and started having a bath. Even from where I was sitting I could smell lavender again.

"Why do you smell like lavender? Where have you been sleeping?"

"At home!" he said, mumbling through a mouthful of fur.

"In a giant bowl of lavender at home?"

Adams ignored me and continued his bath. He wasn't there for long, though. The moment he heard footsteps coming up the stairs, he ran under the desk and vanished. Carter opened the door without knocking.

When I'd seen him two nights ago he was unshaven and looking sad, but it had been night and I hadn't fully grasped the severity of the situation.

His eyes were red like he hadn't slept for days. He was wearing his arm in a sling that had food stains on it. His stubble was now on its way to being a very scraggly beard that simply looked terrible. He had a pallor to his skin that no amount of sun could fix.

"I have some information for you," he said.

He fumbled with his satchel for a moment before I jumped up to help him. He reached inside and pulled out three thick folders, which he put on my desk.

"Property transaction records and a few other things I found," he said. "I've had a look, but I'd like you to read them and see if you find what I did."

I absolutely do not get along with Carter on any level whatsoever, putting him right up there with Hattie in terms of most annoying person in Harlot Bay, but he appeared so broken I couldn't help myself.

"Are you okay?" I asked.

"No, I'm not. Coldwell is going ahead with the eviction."

"Why is he doing that?"

"Because his family is the devil."

I helped him put his satchel on. He said he'd see me in a few days and trudged out.

I sat on the sofa and started looking through the papers, but I wasn't really seeing them. Could it really be as simple as Coldwell being behind the fires? Was he targeting Carter because Carter had been investigating? Or was it merely because Coldwell was actually a bad person? Given my last interaction with him when he came into the office, it seemed he was very bent on ending the free rent program, but that didn't mean he was a criminal.

I mean, there was a little pleasure in the idea that Coldwell was behind it and that we would somehow catch him. It would be glorious to prove that he had burned down that house and warehouse. I'd love to see the look on Detective Moreland's face. Not to mention it would be a relief for me and my family.

I'd finally managed to get myself to concentrate on the papers, mostly land transfer documents, when my cousins and Kira came racing up the stairs to my office.

"There's another one of those strings!" Kira exclaimed.

"We can see them too!" Luce said.

"Let's go investigate!" Molly added.

"Is that a good idea? If we're seen again in another place that burns down, we're going to be in serious trouble."

Molly waved her hands at me as though brushing away my concerns.

"Yes, but we go there and then catch the arsonist and then you're let off scot-free," she said.

A sudden thought occurred to me.

"Did you close down the coffee shop for this?"

"They're doing some renovations," Luce said. "So it is a good time to go investigating."

I looked at the papers, which may as well have had *boring* written all over them.

"Okay, but let's make sure we're not being tailed by anyone, if that's possible."

"I have it covered," Molly said.

At first when they stepped into the room, I couldn't see the red lines, but after a minute of being near Kira, they appeared. Amongst the various colors there was a new line, deep red and vibrating gently. A red line emerged from me and tangled up with it. Kira had one coming from her doing the same. There were none connected to Molly and Luce.

"So weird it's just you two," Luce said, waving her hand through the lines.

We locked up the office and went to Molly's car. She took a deep breath and cast a concealment spell over the entire car.

Normally I would say this was an incredibly stupid thing to do. The more people you have looking at you the more energy it takes. Basically, if you try disappear in a crowd it could exhaust you so badly you pass out within five seconds. Somehow, Molly seemed fine. I felt the concealment ripple around us and then she started the engine and we took off.

"How are you not unconscious right now?" I asked, seeing the tourists filling the streets.

"Slight modification of the spell. People can see us if they're not *interested* in seeing us. The spell only affects anyone who might be watching us deliberately."

I was impressed with that until she gave a gigantic yawn about half a second later and blinked sleepily at the road. We turned a few corners and then Molly waved the spell away, shaking herself to wake up.

This time the line led directly to what you would very charitably call the lower socioeconomic end of Harlot Bay. The houses in this part of town were quite cute, and some of them were large because they were built a very long time ago, but on the whole the entire area was rusting and broken down. There were even a few abandoned houses. I was sure that the red line was going to end in one.

Sure enough, we soon pulled up out in front of an old wreck of a house. The gardens were overgrown and there was a thick hedge blocking most the view. There was no one in sight, so we didn't bother casting another concealment spell. We went through the rusty front gate and up to the house. The hedge wall blocked anyone on the street from seeing us. Molly knocked on the door, but no one answered. She quickly declared the house was obviously abandoned. Luce cast an unlocking spell and soon we were inside, standing at the foot of some stairs where the red line terminated.

"This place would burn like crazy," Luce said, looking around.

It appeared that whoever had been living here had moved out without taking many of their possessions with them. Every room was filled with ancient furniture. It seemed they'd been halfway through packing before they'd left. There were piles of ancient boxes sitting everywhere, some of them half-filled. Underneath the staircase there was a small room where it looked like they'd collected every newspaper and receipt they'd ever received and put them in a big flammable pile.

"Shall we take a look around?" Molly asked.

Molly and Luce went off together to explore upstairs and Kira and I took the bottom floor. The house wasn't creepy like the creepy murder house where we'd placed the, beacon but rather just dusty and abandoned. It felt like a family had possibly lived there at some point. I don't know what would have led them to leave the house with only part of their possessions. There weren't any signs of anything bad.

We went through lots of drawers and cupboards but didn't find anything unusual. There were old electricity bills in one, carryout menus in another. Molly and Luce returned from upstairs and reported that there was nothing interesting up there. Just more boxes and newspapers stacked around the place.

We reconvened in the dusty lounge room, taking our places on the sofa and chairs after whacking them to ensure no spiders were hiding.

"So, what we do now? A stakeout?" Molly asked.

"I guess the arsonist can't burn it down if we're here. Perhaps we'll catch them," I said.

"What if it's a fire spirit, though? Will we even see it?" Luce asked.

I shrugged. I hadn't asked Aunt Cass what exactly a fire spirit looked like. In my mind it was a flame with a happy face, like something out of Japanese anime. In reality it could look like anything, including being totally invisible. For all I knew, the splotch of dirt in the corridor could be it.

"We could stay here and see if anything happens," Luce said.

Lacking any other ideas, we did exactly that. Molly parked her car around the corner in case something did happen.

There was essentially nothing to do in the old house, so we mostly ended up talking and spending time with our phones. We played a variety of word games and things like that, and after the day dragged on for a million years, it was eventually dinnertime and we were all getting hungry.

"Should we go home?" Luce asked at about seven o'clock.

"If this place is going to burn down, one of us needs to be here," I said.

The red line was still deep and dark, terminating at the foot of the stairs. We agreed that we would stay, and Molly and Luce went off to grab some takeout. They were gone almost forty-five minutes before they returned with delicious Indian food and gossip.

"We saw my mother! We think she was meeting someone," Molly said before stuffing some naan in her mouth.

"We'd just bought the takeout, and we saw her walking down the street in the distance. She jumped into this car we didn't recognize and drove away. We didn't see who was in the driver's seat, but it was *definitely* a man," Luce said.

Months ago, Molly had come to believe that her mother was possibly having an affair. She suspected it was with Sheriff Hardy at the time. We'd followed Aunt Ro until we lost her trail one night and since then we hadn't really uncovered any evidence that she was seeing anyone, so we'd let it go.

"Mom said that she's been acting extra spiky recently, which we all know is true. You think it could be about this mystery man?" I asked.

"No doubt about it. If she's cheerful tomorrow, then we definitely know something is going on," Molly said.

"Your mom has a secret boyfriend?" Kira asked, giggling.

"We think so. And we would only use that information against her in the most loving way," Molly replied.

"You could put a magical tracker on her car," Kira said.

"What's a magical tracker?" Luce asked.

Over dinner Kira explained the concept of a magical tracker. It was almost the same as the beacons Kira and I had placed around town. You stuck it on whatever you wanted to track, like a car, and then cast a spell on it. It was such a low-level spell it would be practically impossible to detect against the background magic in Harlot Bay.

"The only problem is you need a certain type of crystal," Kira explained.

"Who taught you that?" I asked.

"My grandma, actually. She taught me a few cool things."

It was the first time I'd heard Kira talk about Hattie without sarcasm. Obviously living with her was not fun, but I guess that's the thing with relationships: there might be bad but there is usually some good. Once more, it occurred to me that I really wished there actually were schools for witches, but that's not the way it worked. Magic is a personal thing taught from witch to witch. What works for one doesn't always work for another. Our moms and Aunt Cass had taught us plenty of things, but there was lots they hadn't.

We finished dinner and then kept talking about all kinds of things together as the night wore on. But we soon realized our mistake. Were we actually planning on sleeping here? Sure, there were beds, but there was no bedding. The prospect of staying up all night together wasn't appealing.

"We could stay here and then you guys could come back after midnight and relieve us?" Molly offered.

"Yeah, I guess," I said. It wasn't the best plan, but what else could we do? If we all went home and then the house burned down, we'd lose the opportunity to catch either the person or the fire spirit that was the cause.

Kira and I took Molly's car and drove home with an agreement to come back at two a.m. There was no family dinner again tonight (no guests) so Kira and I watched television and talked with Adams. At least today he wasn't smelling so much of lavender.

Before it got too late, I set my alarm and went to bed, starting to feel excited that tomorrow I'd be having a lunch date with Jack.

It seemed I'd hardly closed my eyes when I woke up to my alarm. It was one thirty in the morning.

I looked in on Kira, who was fast asleep, and almost decided to leave her there. Then I realized if I were at the house by myself and something went wrong, I might need some help. Besides, I needed someone to keep me awake. So I woke her up. We had some coffee and then drove back to the house.

We met a very tired Molly and Luce. The house hadn't burned down and they hadn't heard anyone or anything unusual. Kira and I both spent the first hour sitting on our phones, doing anything we could to entertain ourselves and stay awake. It was around three in the morning that the red line that had terminated at the foot of the stairs pulled away, out the front door.

"Did your Slip magic disappear?" I asked.

"No, something else is happening," Kira said. We rushed outside to see the red line retracting down the street like fishing line being wound in. It vanished around the corner so quickly that we knew there was no point in chasing it. Even if we had a car we probably wouldn't catch up.

"What do you think happened?" I asked, looking up and down the darkened street. There were still other lines faintly shimmering in the darkness, but no red ones that felt like they were fire.

"Maybe whatever it was changed its mind?" Kira said.

Now the big question was whether we stayed in the house for the rest of the night. With the line gone, it felt like this place definitely wouldn't burn down, but then what if we went home and then the red line returned?

Despite the fact I could hear my soft bed calling me from all the way up on the hill, we reluctantly decided to stay in the house until morning. Kira ended up falling asleep, but I managed to stay awake until the sun rose. The house didn't burn down, and I called Molly and Luce to pick us up.

CHAPTER FOURTEEN

*K*ira and I ate breakfast before going to sleep. I guess this is one of the advantages of being self-employed and having a failing business: if you need a nap, you can have one. Besides, today was my lunch date with Jack, and there was no way I'd be turning up with giant bags under my eyes.

I woke up around ten and quickly got myself together to head into town. I still had Carter's papers to read through and also didn't want to miss Jack if he arrived early. I checked in on Kira before I left, but she wasn't in her bed. Aunt Cass wasn't down at the main part of the house, either.

I was tired and driving along in a somewhat bleary way, the air-conditioning on full blast, when I came to a halt at a stop sign. There was a lot of traffic (tourists), so I sat there looking left and right until I happened to see a familiar shape in the window of the house on the corner.

It was Adams!

A rosy-cheeked woman with graying hair was scratching him under the chin.

What the hell?

I quickly found somewhere to park, suddenly understanding why my cat smelled like lavender all the time. I marched up to the house, which was a modern white-walled place, two stories with a beautiful garden. I stopped at the window and saw Adams sleeping on a white sofa. The woman was nowhere to be seen, so I rapped on the window and he jerked awake. The moment he saw me, he jumped off the sofa and dived behind it.

"I can see you!" I called out.

"No, you can't!" Adams said from behind the sofa.

I banged my knuckles on the glass.

"You are in so much trouble, mister," I said.

I knocked on the front door. A few minutes later, the owner of the house opened it.

"Yes? How can I help you?" she asked.

"Hi, you have a cat in there sleeping on your sofa who I think belongs to me."

From where I was standing I could see Adams' black paws behind the sofa. He was hiding and keeping silent.

"Oh, do you mean Rodrigo? He's been visiting for years."

"Rodrigo? That's his name?"

"Oh yes, we first met him about ten years ago when we'd returned from a vacation in Spain. He came in meowing like he'd never eaten in his life. It was raining and the poor thing was shivering from cold. So we started feeding him. He probably comes by every second day."

"Really? That's fascinating," I said, trying to stop myself from gritting my teeth. "I guess maybe I must be wrong, then. He looks *so* much like my cat at home. Actually, my cat is quite heavy and so we've been forced to put him on a diet recently. For example, we had to declare just this morning that he's not getting any more cheese for quite a long time."

Adams poked his head out from behind the sofa, a look of

horror on his furry face. The moment the old lady looked at him, I drew my finger across my throat and gave him a glare.

"Oh, this one loves cheese. I think we go through about a block a week," she said.

With the door open I became aware of the scent of lavender floating out. There were potpourri bowls spread everywhere throughout the house.

"Sorry to bother you. I'm going to pick up some diet cat food for my cat, who is going on a severe diet the moment I get home," I said, directing most of my comments to the furry feet behind the sofa.

The lady said goodbye to me and then I walked back to my car. When I got in, Adams emerged from under the passenger-side seat, yawning like he'd been asleep.

"Good morning," Adams yawned, showing me his white teeth. "I must have fallen asleep in the car."

"Oh, really? That's how you're going to play it? I didn't just see you sitting on the sofa in that house, *Rodrigo?*"

Adams sat on the passenger seat and started washing himself.

"I've been asleep under the seat the whole time. Is there another cat in there who looks exactly like me? Is he handsome too?"

"Yes, there is another cat in there who looks *exactly* like you. And he's going on a diet."

"A diet? Why would you put me on a diet? I mean him."

"Because you need to lose weight. You've been sneaking off to eat cheese at other people's houses. Is your name even Adams? Or is it Rodrigo? Julio? Emilio?"

"You shouldn't be mean to hungry cats," Adams said sulkily.

I knew I wouldn't be able to get very far with him. Lying cats were even worse than teenagers. A teenager will flatly deny things even in the face of overwhelming evidence, but a cat would literally steal the cheese out of your hand in front of you and then claim that he'd never eaten or stolen anything in his entire life. Still, I had to make it clear to him that it wasn't exactly safe to keep visiting the same people for such a long time.

"I know you might like seeing them. But if you visit the same people for such a long period of time and you don't look like you age, then they're going to get suspicious."

"I only visit people for ten years," he mumbled.

"What? So even when we weren't living here, you were visiting?"

"I'm allowed to visit!"

Adams, being a magical cat, has the strange ability to show up in unexpected places. I leave him at home when I go to work and I often get a call from the moms telling me he's in the Big Pie storeroom or somewhere else he shouldn't be. I had no idea if he could somehow transport across entire states, though.

I pulled out my phone to check the time. It was now almost eleven and looked like I wouldn't get much work in before Jack arrived for lunch. Adams took this opportunity to leap up and shout into the phone "Call PETA!"

What he didn't know was I actually have a Peta stored in my phone, an old friend who had moved away. We're mostly now only email and online friends. The phone dialed and picked up before I could stop it.

"Hey, Harlow!" Peta said.

"She's starving a little black cat!" Adams called out.

I shushed him quite severely, putting my hand over his mouth and pulling the phone away.

"What was that? Did someone shout out something about a cat?" Peta asked.

"Oh, hey, Peta, it was Molly being silly. Sorry I accidentally dialed you."

"That's okay. We should actually talk soon anyway, catch up."

I promised Peta that we would, then hung up. I shoved my phone in my pocket before I let Adams go.

"Calling Peta isn't going to help you," I told him.

"They protect animals great and small," Adams said, quoting an advertisement that he'd seen once.

I didn't have the time to explain to a greedy little cat the difference between PETA and Peta, so I let it go.

By the time I got to work, Adams was snoozing on the passenger seat. He wanted to stay in the car, so I put the window down and told him to stay out of sight.

The remaining hour until lunch seemed to drag interminably. I tried to distract myself by reading through Carter's papers, but it was all boring property transfers and none of them were in order. Some were from the 1950s, some the 1970s, a bunch from the 1930s mixed up with the 1980s. Properties would appear, but with misspelled street names and mixed-up lot numbers.

I wasn't entirely sure what I was actually supposed to learn. Coldwell had bought properties that had burned down and so had other real estate developers. I didn't need evidence to prove that.

I was sorting through the papers when there was a knock on the door. I looked up, grinning, but it wasn't Jack. It was Jonas.

"Hey, Jonas," I said, feeling my heart sink just a little. Jonas is a good guy, but he was not the one I was waiting to see.

"Hi, Harlow. My dorkus of a brother has just called me from down the street, where he is buying a new shirt because he got paint all over the one he was wearing to lunch. He will be here in about five minutes. Do you guys not have each other's numbers yet?"

"We seem to have missed that. I don't really know why."

Jonas ran his hand through his hair and then rubbed his stubbly jawline.

"Do you have a minute so I can ask you some questions about some of the people in town? I've had some stuff happen lately and I don't know if it's normal or not," Jonas asked.

I waved him to the sofa.

"Step into my office. Weird happenings in Harlot Bay is my department," I quipped.

Jonas sat on the sofa next to Carter's pile of papers which I'd left sitting open. He looked down and saw the property transfer papers that had Coldwell printed on them.

"This is weird. I was about to ask you about Sylvester Coldwell. What do you know about him?"

"He's a Harlot Bay real estate developer, one of many, from a family that has been here for a long time. I'm looking into whether there is any connection between fires in the past and real estate development purchases. I don't know if he's a friend of yours, but I think he's sleazy and horrible and I don't like him whatsoever."

Jonas smiled and raised his eyebrows.

"That's pretty much what I wanted to know. I had both him and Dominic Gresso coming to my office trying to get me involved in real estate development with them. I happened to buy these three really old houses over near where that warehouse burned down a couple of nights ago and have had both of them offering to buy them from me. I also had Dominic Gresso in here making big noises about referring work to each other and things like that. But at the same time, he implied that I was small fish in a big pond and he was the big fish. He was kind of a jerk."

"Yup, that's Dominic. His family has been here a long time too. My Aunt Cass doesn't like him because when he was twelve he went around saying he was selling cookies and she put in her order, which he never delivered."

"Nondelivery of cookies? That's a rookie mistake, especially in a small town. Stuff like that will follow you forever," Jonas said. "So, what is all this here?" he asked, pointing at the pile of land transfers.

I told him I'd received them from Carter Wilkins and that it was background information on all the land transfers that had occurred over a number of decades.

"I haven't found anything suspicious yet, but I'll keep looking."

"So you're saying that I should stay away from both these guys?"

"I wouldn't trust either of them farther than you can throw them."

"Hello?" I heard Jack call from downstairs. My heart leapt at the sound.

"Five dollars says he started painting without realizing he was wearing a nice shirt," Jonas said to me as Jack came up the stairs.

Jack walked into the office wearing what was clearly a new shirt, given it still had price tags hanging off it. He noticed and snapped them off before shoving them in his pocket.

"Let me guess… you were at the house and you decided to pick up a paintbrush even though you had no intention of painting and a second later you had paint on yourself?" Jonas asked.

"Yes, and?" Jack said, rolling his eyes at his brother but still smiling.

Jonas turned to me. "Our dad handed down many gifts to us – great hair, wonderful eyes, sense of humor. Well, I mean, only *one* of us really got most of the gifts, but he also handed over the gift of starting work in inappropriate clothing. Dad would go to a building site to check something, pick up a paintbrush or a hammer and start working. It's a real problem. They're thinking of naming a syndrome after our family."

Jack stuck his tongue out at his brother, who clapped him on the shoulder as he went by and out the door.

"Ready for lunch? Or are you going to be spending some time today being a fugitive from justice?"

Obviously Jack knew I had been taken in for questioning and he was trying to joke about it, but for some reason the smile slipped away from my face.

"I'm sorry. Too soon? Come with me to lunch," Jack said.

I recovered my smile when I kissed him.

We went to a small Indian place two streets away called Curry Cauldron. I know it sounds like eating hot curry in the middle of summer is ridiculous, but the Curry Cauldron is well-known for its incredibly good air-conditioning. It was like stepping into a meat locker, and I swear I could see a plume of my breath in front of me.

We found a small table in a darkened nook and I decided to dive into the subject of me and the police and get it over and done with.

"I did get taken in for questioning about the fires in Harlot Bay. And I'm pretty sure most of the town knows," I said over my menu.

The butter naan looked good.

"I heard there's a special investigator in town. Why did you go in to have an interview with him? Hasn't the Internet taught you anything about talking to the cops?" Jack said with a teasing smile.

"Are you saying I need to watch what I say to you?" I teased in return.

"I'm sure I could make you crack under questioning. Also, former policeman. I'm all *for* crime now."

I knew I was in that ridiculous romantic space when he could practically say anything and it would sound devilishly charming, but I couldn't help being charmed. We'd had a great date at Valhalla Viking, although it had been cut a little short by the hedge fire that had pulled me to it. Now it was the middle of the day, and I was hoping against hope that there wouldn't be another fire.

"I know I probably shouldn't have talked to him..." I began. We ordered some food (lamb rogan josh, butter naan, mango lassi) and while we waited I told Jack about the fires I'd been involved in. The bad wiring at the apartment building and at the house on our land. Zero Bend leaving a kettle on the stove. I stopped short of telling him about the fire at the lighthouse. Only Sheriff Hardy knew about that. Although, Carter Wilkins had caught us soaking wet from where we'd flown our broomstick into the ocean and I guess suspected that we'd been involved. Thus far he hadn't printed anything about it. Actually, now that I think about it, it *was* strange that he hadn't pursued the story. I wonder if Sheriff Hardy had dissuaded him?

Jack asked a few questions here and there. The delicious food arrived and we ate.

I told him about going out to the warehouse because I suspected that empty places were being burned down, and the coincidence that it *did* burn down. I felt like I could trust him, but of course I could never reveal that I was a witch. I mean, if we ended up together, *eventually* I would have to tell the truth. Just like Molly and Luce would tell Will and Ollie at some point. But that was a secret to be revealed another day very much in the future.

By the time I'd finished the story, Jack's voice had turned grave.

"It doesn't look good. There is a lot of circumstantial evidence and people have gone to jail for less. The good thing is that you're not guilty. I know it sounds obvious, but you're not the arsonist and that means they won't find any evidence of you where there has been a fire. If you really want to seal the deal, you should probably go away for a month. The fact that there could be a fire while you're gone means you didn't do it, unless of course you have an accomplice."

"The only accomplice I have is a little black cat who eats too much cheese."

"Oh, a little black cat, did you say? That changes everything. You're definitely going down for this. Everyone knows that black cats are pyromaniacs. Why are you protecting him? What do you and that cat have against Harlot Bay?" Jack said, grinning at me.

We finished our lunch, changing topics to what he was working on. He'd taken a renovation job working for a little old lady who wanted to modernize her kitchen.

"Actually, you should see her house and library. It's really amazing. Do you want to check it out? It's only three streets away. She's off visiting friends while I work," Jack said.

"So someone told you I have a weakness for books?"

"Do you? Well, then, let's definitely go to this library right now!"

I laughed, the sudden thought of kissing Jack in someone else's library coming into my mind. I knew it was absurd, but at the same time it felt like something I very much wanted to do.

We got out of there and went to Jack's truck, which was parked nearby. It still smelled of leather and man and sawdust. We drove the three streets and parked. Jack wasn't wrong. It was really a mansion, with giant marble pillars and a balcony. The garden was simply spectacular and filled with colorful plants and rows of thyme and rosemary. Bees lazily bobbed about.

"Come in and check this out," Jack said, leading me to the house. He opened the door and we went inside, entering into a cavernous hallway with gleaming polished wooden floors.

"Wow," I breathed. I followed him in through to the kitchen, which was clearly being renovated. There were sheets all over the floor to stop any drips of paint, and the cabinets all along one wall had been disassembled. Nearby, there was also a wall freshly painted in light cream. I noticed for the first time that Jack had a few dots of that on his boots.

"So Jonas was right? You were in here doing something else and then you picked up a paintbrush?"

"I stopped by to grab some timber measurements and then I saw the wall. I thought I'd test the paint to see whether it looked good against the cabinets. And... then I got paint on myself," Jack explained.

He grabbed my hand and pulled me through to the library.

Oh. My. Goddess.

Floor-to-ceiling shelves. A library ladder. Comfy single chairs and tasteful small wooden tables. A translucent green vase of flowers almost glowing in the light coming through the window.

"Muh," I said, trying to take it all in.

"Nice, huh."

"Muh," I repeated. So many beautiful hardcover books.

"Okay, gotta get back to work now, so I'll take you back to your office," Jack said, touching me on the shoulders.

I hadn't kissed him yet, so I took this opportunity to step a little closer and smiled at him. Jack did the same and then kissed me in front of the collected works of Charles Dickens. The kiss went on for longer than I anticipated, and by the time we pulled apart, my heart was thudding in my chest. I knew if I didn't get out of there soon I might do something that I hadn't planned on doing. Note, I did *not* say do something that I would *regret*. I was certain I would not regret it. Nevertheless... we'd hardly dated at all, and so I cleared my throat, straightened my clothes and smiled at Jack before telling him it was time for me to go to my office. He drove me back, both of us casting sideways glances at each other. I felt like I was a teenager again, out on a date my parents didn't know about.

Outside my office, I kissed him goodbye, the urge to keep kissing him strongly pulling at me. I finally managed to break away and get out of his truck. It was a hot day, but Jack's cheeks were slightly more flushed than the heat warranted. Jack winked at me and I winked back before he was gone, leaving me surrounded by tourists, floating off my feet.

CHAPTER FIFTEEN

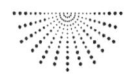

"And then what happened?" Luce said, her hands clenched in front of her like she was praying.

"And then we kissed in front of the library," I said.

Molly, Luce, and Kira gave three united *squees* together.

Apparently Jack driven us past Traveler and I'd been so caught up in going over to the house with him that I hadn't even noticed. My cousins and Kira with their eagle eyes had spotted me. They'd known I was having a lunch date with Jack, but then seeing us driving off together was a whole 'nother thing.

"Did he take his shirt off and do any work?" Molly asked.

"No, we only kissed, it was perfectly innocent," I said, somewhat censoring my story. If Kira hadn't been there, I might have told the whole truth. I didn't want her to get the idea that I had gone boy-mad.

The analysis of my love life was cut short by Ollie arriving at the front door. He and Molly were going out tonight. For the first time in a while, Luce and Will weren't going with them. Molly kissed him welcome but then raced off to get ready. She'd been so caught up in my story of my date that she still hadn't changed out of her sweaty coffee clothes.

Kira moved herself over to the kitchen table, tapping away on her phone and casting sideways glances at Ollie. As I've said before, I do not have the slightest bit of romantic interest in my cousin's boyfriends, but both of them are damn cute boys.

"So how's the library going?" I asked Ollie after we'd taken a seat on the sofa.

"Not much happening. Mainly helping Carter Wilkins try to find old records."

"Was that you who retrieved all the property transfer records? He gave them to me to look through."

"Yeah, I gave him most of them. The council abandoned its archives after a certain point, so the library ended up with them. There's another entire warehouse full of old papers in desperate need of being digitized, but they're doing all the police records first."

Sheriff Hardy had told me that the police were slowly moving over to the modern world, but there were decades of old files waiting to be scanned and transferred. I'd written a story on it for my newspaper. The whole process was moving incredibly slowly due to budget cuts. In most towns the sheriff had his own building, but to save money, in Harlot Bay his office was in the same building as the police station.

"From what I hear, you're going to be waiting awhile."

"Why are you looking at property transfers?" Ollie asked.

I told him about the fires in town that had occurred all throughout our history and how there was a suspicion that a local real estate developer was possibly profiting in some way. By the time I was finished, Ollie was nodding his head rapidly and his face was lit up.

"You know, I've been thinking the same thing. I've been writing a post for my website about the historical fires of

Harlot Bay and as I was researching it, I realized a lot of the new buildings had been built on the sites of suspicious fires. It almost always comes down to the Gresso family or Coldwell. I understand that they are the two biggest real estate developers in town and so it appears perfectly legal and aboveboard, but if you look at it another way, they have profited enormously from these so-called accidental fires. I read a journal entry where someone claimed they'd been asked to sell their home by Coldwell and when they refused, their business burned down a few days later. It put them under financial strain, and so they were forced to sell."

I looked across at Luce and Kira and I could see they were thinking the same thing. Was there something suspicious going on? Or was it a fire spirit?

"Have you found any evidence that there is an arsonist in town right now?" Ollie asked me.

"Well, I had a suspicion that an arsonist was burning down abandoned buildings. I happened to go to one a few days ago that then got burnt down that very night. Then, of course, I got called in for questioning."

"Questioning? What happened?"

Did he not know? I was so used to my cousins blabbing every single detail of our lives that I'd automatically assumed that Ollie would know I had been taken in for police questioning.

I gave him a summary of there being an arson investigator in town and told him I'd gone in for questioning because I'd been at the addresses of some places that had burnt down, coincidentally. By the time I'd given my brief explanation, Ollie was looking very grim.

"Maybe you shouldn't investigate this further," he said. "Did you know that there have been some journalists who have died in Harlot Bay as well?"

Molly came out of her bedroom looking like a million

bucks, wearing a red polka-dot dress. Even looking amazing, she couldn't distract Ollie as he told me of the coincidental deaths of journalists in Harlot Bay. The most recent deaths were in the 1980s of two journalists who had been investigating fires in Harlot Bay.

"The first one was ruled an accidental drowning, given they found excessive amounts of alcohol in her blood. But there was always a suspicion it was murder. For starters, a friend of hers reported she was afraid of water, to the point that she never went swimming or anywhere near the ocean. So why would she get drunk and then hop in some random rowboat to try to make her way across to Truer Island? The second one was suicide. He hung himself, even though his friend said he never expressed any suicidal thoughts and in fact only two weeks earlier he'd bought a new house. He'd been packing at the time and then apparently just decided to make a noose and hang himself off his back porch."

"So you're saying there was some murderer from the 1980s who killed journalists who were investigating fires and now Harlow is investigating fires and someone is going to kill her!" Luce said.

"I hope not. But between that and some other deaths that have occurred even further back for journalists, maybe it's something you should give up on. Let it go, get out of town until they find who it is, and then think about coming back," Ollie said.

"Okay, I think that's enough murder talk for tonight, honey," Molly said, grabbing Ollie by the arm. She hustled him out. As soon as Ollie was gone, Kira disappeared to her room.

"This sounds really bad," Luce said.

"Hey, it's being a journalist, this kind of thing happens," I said.

"If you're a journalist making a lot of money, then I might

be able to agree with you. But for the kind of cash you're pulling in, it's just not worth it."

It was so true that it didn't even sting, not even a little.

We were coming up on a family dinner that Molly had gotten out of so Luce went to the bathroom to get ready. I spend the rest of the time looking through the papers Carter had given me. In amongst the property transfer documents, I found a list of fires and whether there were any victims. One caught my eye – about ten years ago, a house had burned down and a woman had been killed. I actually remembered that happening. I think the only reason it wasn't big news for the town was that the same day, a tourist had fallen down the cliffs and broken both his legs and a hip.

Luce emerged from the bathroom, sitting next to me on the sofa to put her shoes on.

"Did you borrow my blue cardigan?" she asked.

"I don't think so."

"Do you know the one I mean? It has a rose stitched on the front."

"I know it. I haven't seen it."

"Maybe I left it at Will's house... I feel like half my clothes are missing. Can't seem to find anything," Luce mumbled to herself.

Once she was ready, we all walked down to the main house. Aunt Cass, who was usually in her chair watching police shows, was nowhere to be seen. In the kitchen the moms were laughing and chatting as they made dinner. We took our places and talked a bit with Luce about the renovations at Traveler while we waited.

"I'm thinking we all go to the beach when we have to shut down," Luce said.

"That could be good," I said.

"I love the beach," Kira added.

I had no doubt that she loved the beach. I'd been letting

her off to go there rather than work and I was sure that Luce's teasing had some truth: Kira probably did have a secret boyfriend.

Aunt Ro came rushing out of the kitchen, her cheeks glowing and wearing a wide smile. She placed a silver platter in the center of the table and beamed at us.

"Dinner is ready," she trilled.

I tried to hold it in, and I guess Luce and Kira did too, but we all failed. I started giggling and so did they. Obviously Aunt Ro had a secret someone on the side and clearly had met up with them last night. I wondered who was the mysterious man?

"You seem very happy today," Luce said.

"Yes, you seem incredibly relaxed," Kira added, deadpan.

I couldn't take it any longer. I broke out laughing.

"What are you talking about? You girls..." Aunt Ro said. She practically danced her way back to the kitchen. If she'd done a pirouette it wouldn't have been out of place.

"I can't wait to tell Molly about this," Luce said.

It felt good to laugh in spite of all the terrible things that had happened around us recently. Aunt Ro having a possible new boyfriend meant we could sneak around to find him, tease her about it, and if it came to it, throw her to the wolves (also known as the rest of the family) in case the other moms turned on us. It was perfect.

Aunt Cass emerged from the lounge room and grumpily stomped her way to her position at the head of the table. She hadn't been in there before – did she have a secret door out there?

"Whattup, C-Money?" Kira said and held up a hand.

Aunt Cass glanced at her and then reluctantly gave her the high five she was waiting for. She turned to Luce.

"Where's the wine?" she said, picking up an empty glass.

Luce rushed off and returned with two bottles a moment later.

"Red or white?"

"Alcohol, lots of it, now," Aunt Cass said. Luce filled her glass with white wine, which Aunt Cass downed almost instantly. She then shook the glass for Luce to fill again.

"Are you okay?" I asked. Yes, I was the one who was going to be the sacrificial lamb in case Aunt Cass exploded.

"I can't work out what is starting the fires in town. The beacons aren't working properly and it's incredibly frustrating."

"Can we help you at all?" Luce asked.

"You can help me by keeping that wine flowing," Aunt Cass said, taking another gulp.

"You told me the most important thing for a Slip Witch is to maintain equilibrium," Kira said.

"I know I said that. But someone died in one of those fires, and unless we work out how to stop it I think someone is going to die again. I don't want to talk about it."

The tone in her voice was enough to make us all stop asking questions immediately.

Aunt Ro and the moms emerged from the kitchen, laughing and chatting, carrying silver platters with them. They put them down on the table and then revealed glistening roast lamb, thyme-roasted potatoes, honey carrots, green beans and a bacon, garlic and spring onion gravy.

We all dug in and for a change no one sniped at each other. I was happy about that, given this was probably one of the few remaining family dinners that we would have without any guests present. Now that the website was working properly, bookings had come rushing in, and in a few days the Torrent Mansion Bed-and-Breakfast would be full.

It seemed that Aunt Ro's happiness was infectious and we

were talking and laughing through dinner. All except Aunt Cass, of course, who'd retreated to single grunts and then not even that. She soon stopped eating food and stuck to drinking wine.

Just as we were getting to the end of dinner, Aunt Freya pointed her finger at me and said, "You need to keep your little black cat out of our kitchen."

"Oh no, what has he done now?"

"What *hasn't* he done? An entire loaf of bread went missing. Also, cheese, fruit, biscuits from the pantry. I swear he should be the size of the house. He's eating enough for a whole person."

"You have no idea," I said. I told them all about "Rodrigo" and his visits, where he slept on a white sofa and was fed blocks of cheese, apparently.

"I would bet he's visiting a lot more families as well. Probably operating under multiple aliases."

"Give that little guy a break. He is very adorable, and what does it matter if he visits lots of families? Cats are wonderful and they bring a lot of joy to a lot of people. He shouldn't eat all the food, but it's still a good thing that he's doing," Aunt Ro said.

Luce and I exchanged a glance and I giggled again before clearing my throat.

"Are you talking about the same little black cat that only a few days ago you said was going to be made into a bathmat if you caught him in the pizza oven again? The same little black cat that you once threatened to turn into an oven mitt?"

"Well, I wasn't feeling very good then, but I'm feeling much happier now," Aunt Ro said.

That was it. Luce, Kira and I burst out into laughter and couldn't stop ourselves. The moms just looked at us, puzzled. We couldn't tell them what we knew.

"You should tell other people the joke," Mom said, pointing her butter knife at me.

"I will, I will, one day," I gasped, my stomach hurting from laughing too much.

After dinner we returned to our end of the mansion and I told Adams he had to cut back on his food theft from the main kitchen. He denied everything, of course.

"Hey, I'm just passing the message along. If you don't want to get turned into a bathmat, maybe you should *not* eat all the biscuits in the cupboard."

Adams jumped up on Kira's lap and started kneading at her T-shirt.

"Can you write an email to PETA for me?" he asked, starting to dribble already. Kira laughed and scratched him behind the ears.

CHAPTER SIXTEEN

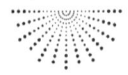

In the morning I was feeling pretty good. It wasn't official or anything, but I kinda had a boyfriend. Happy dance!

So did Luce and Molly, and so did Aunt Ro, it seemed. Yes, there were still plenty of things wrong, like Aunt Cass not being able to track down the source of the fires and also me possibly being a suspect, but right now, after a good dinner last night and an even better night of sleep, I was feeling pretty great.

That feeling barely lasted past breakfast, when Detective Moreland pulled up at the front of the house. I debated hiding in my bedroom, but he'd seen me through the front window, so I reluctantly went to the front door.

Detective Moreland was still wearing his standard-issue police uniform and had that notebook out again.

"Can you tell me where you were last night?" he asked.

Despite my own warnings to myself about never ever talking to the police, I was certain I had a foolproof alibi this time.

"I had dinner with my family and then came back here and went to bed."

"You didn't go anywhere last night?"

"No, why?"

"Did you go to an address on Anderson Lane yesterday?"

"Um…" I said, trying to remember. Before I could say anything more and possibly land myself in jail, Jack came driving up the hill and parked his truck next to Detective Moreland's car.

He got out of the truck and called out, "Don't answer any more questions!" before walking over.

"Jack Bishop. Have you decided to answer some questions for me?" Detective Moreland said.

"No comment."

"What's this about?" I asked. We were interrupted again by Molly racing up the driveway and pulling to a stop next to Jack's truck. She was going somewhat faster than he had been. Pieces of gravel scattered across the road and a cloud of dust rose up.

"What's going on here?" Molly said when she reached the front door.

"Last night a house on Anderson Lane was mostly destroyed by a fire. It started in the kitchen and then engulfed the library and most of the bedrooms. You know the house I'm talking about, don't you, Jack?" Detective Moreland said.

It felt like the world had stopped spinning. Another fire? *Another fire* at a place I'd just been? And now Jack was involved as well? I felt like being sick.

"In case it's not in your records, I only recently got back to town and Harlot Bay's been having fires for a number of weeks now. Perhaps you should look into that and who might benefit from such fires," Jack said. "I think we should all go inside now and let Detective Moreland leave to do some work."

"Good idea," Molly said with a lot of bravado in her voice. Jack came inside and Molly followed, closing the door gently in Detective Moreland's face. He got back in his car and drove away.

As soon as he was gone. Molly turned to me.

"What was he talking about? Were you at a place that burnt down again?"

"I think so. Yesterday Jack took me to see that library I told you about. Last night most of the house burned down."

Jack quickly confirmed that this was the case. Sometime after midnight a fire had started in the kitchen and then spread. The fire brigade had come as fast as possible, but due to the high number of flammable objects in the house, they'd been barely able to contain it.

At the end of Jack's explanation, Luce surprisingly clapped her hands and directed us all to the kitchen table.

"Family conference," she said. "Everyone sit down."

We all sat down, me and Molly feeling a bit mystified. It wasn't really like Luce to take charge like this.

"So someone is targeting Harlow and burning down houses in Harlot Bay. Obviously they started burning down houses first and now that she's gotten involved they're targeting her. It's the same situation that happened back in the 1980s, and that resulted in a lot of houses burnt down and two journalists dead. We don't want that to happen, so let's figure out what to do," Luce said.

"How do you know all this?" Molly asked. "I mean, I know Ollie told you yesterday, but have you found out more since then?"

"He sent me some links to look at, so I was doing research all last night. That's not the point, though. Whoever it is obviously followed Harlow and Jack to that house and then set it on fire that night to make it appear they're involved. Now, I want to hear hypotheses. You first, Scruffy McGreen-BlueEyes," she said, pointing a finger directly at Jack.

I could tell he thought this was weird, but he went with it anyway.

"I think you might be right about someone targeting Harlow. I was looking into some of the fires that happened in the past, and there does seem to be a connection between fires and then journalists being killed. This is going to sound like a big leap, but I think it's the same person or group of people operating over a number of decades. I think the best place to look is where the money goes," Jack said.

"Okay, now you," Luce said, pointing a finger at Kira.

Kira put her hands over her mouth, shocked.

"I don't know anything. I have no idea why the fires are starting. Why are you asking me?" With that, Kira rushed off into her room and slammed the door behind her.

"Teenagers," Molly muttered.

It might be *teenagers*, but also it was witches, and a Slip Witch in particular. In front of Jack, we couldn't reveal that Kira was a Slip Witch who had set napkins on fire with her mind. So we just had to cover it by her being a Moody Teenager.

Luce went around the table, and we each threw in what we knew, what we suspected and wild random guesses.

"How about a traveling band of arsonists who come back to the same town every twenty years?" Luce said.

"You mean like that really dodgy horror movie *The Fire Dwellers*?" Molly asked. "The movie that we watched three weeks ago and you got really scared at?"

"You know fiction mirrors reality. It could be happening here," Luce said.

Molly glanced at her phone and suddenly jumped up from the table.

"We're going to be late," she said to Luce.

She checked the time and followed Molly, bolting away. Within two minutes Jack and I were left facing each other over the kitchen table.

"I know with the journalist murders, you're probably going to say that I should get out of town –" I began. Jack cut me off, shaking his head.

"No, you need to stay here. Someone is doing this and we need to stop them. You're a journalist and you should be able to do your job in safety. I'm going to make sure this person is caught."

I know we'd hardly been dating, but there was a tone in his voice that sent a little thrill through me. It was something along the lines of a man going out to fight a lion to protect his girl.

"You're right," I said, not really sure which part he was right about. Given that I'd been on the brink of closing down the *Harlot Bay Reader* multiple times this month, it was flattering to be called a journalist.

"I'm going to look into Sylvester Coldwell. If don't find anything there, I'm going to move on to Dominic Gresso and then to any other real estate agents and developers I can find in town. I think there's a strong case that one of them is involved. Problem is that we have to stay apart. I'm going to see if I can catch someone following you. We'll have to stay in message contact only."

I don't know what it was... perhaps seeing him so serious? Perhaps that he was looking extra scruffy this morning, but I wanted to leap across the kitchen table and kiss him. I had to stifle that impulse when Kira emerged from her room and went to the kitchen.

"I'm going to work on investigating the agents too. I'll message you," I said.

Then, folks, we did it. A big leap forward. We exchanged phone numbers.

We had a brief kiss then Jack said goodbye to Kira, who just turned red and mumbled something in reply.

Despite what I'd said about not leaving town, it wasn't actually such a bad idea. One thing I was definitely sure of was that Kira and I could not follow any more of those red lines to any addresses. I definitely wasn't going to any house if I didn't have a non-magical reason to be there.

I was putting on my boots (knee-high, it's summer, I don't care) and getting ready to leave for work when Aunt Cass burst into the house.

The grumpy, sullen wine-drinking Aunt Cass from yesterday was gone.

"It's a witch!" she shouted out.

"A witch?"

"She's causing the fires. She's in pain and somewhere in Harlot Bay. She might not be the sole cause, but she is definitely one of them. That's why the beacons weren't working properly," Aunt Cass said triumphantly.

Kira frowned and bit her lip.

"You don't think it's…"

"It's not you. I checked. You're clean, well, as clean as a teenager can be," Aunt Cass said.

Kira let out a sigh of relief.

"If it's a witch, do you know any way we can find her?" I asked.

"I'm going to make a different kind of beacon. One that I think will only find the witch and not get messed up by anything else. It's going to take a few days, though, because I need to wait on delivery of a different type of crystal. Hold tight, keep your eyes open. I think this is going to be over soon."

Aunt Cass zipped out, definitely not looking like a woman in her eighties.

I took Kira to the office with me and set her to work organizing all the property transfer papers into chronological order. She actually did that amazingly quickly and then slumped down on the sofa to spend some quality time with her phone. I dug into Sylvester Coldwell and tried to work out how I could get to speak with anyone he worked with at his office without it being suspicious. It wasn't long, though, before Kira's frequent sighs and fidgeting on the sofa started to get on my nerves.

"Maybe you should work at the bakery today," I said to her.

"Okay, I'll go," Kira said.

"They'll happily feed you, but just in case you don't want delicious carbs, I might have some money," I said, opening my desk drawer. I usually drop the cash that John gives me in there. I was very sure that there was at least sixty dollars the last time I looked, but I couldn't seem to find it. There was nothing more than a few loose coins.

"Sorry, thought I had some cash with me. Eat at the bakery or ask one of the moms for money," I said.

"No, it's okay, I'll eat at the bakery," Kira said hastily, heading for the door at full speed.

My immediate suspicion, of course, was that Kira had stolen the money. She might have seen it when John came in for his counseling session. I knew she'd been having some trouble, but I hadn't been told precisely what it was.

Normal teenage trouble? Stealing money, shoplifting, sneaking out.

Hattie Stern's teenage trouble? I dunno, probably forgetting to flush or wearing a sweater that was too "fancy."

I let the money go. It was a complicated issue and the fact was that I wasn't Kira's mother. I hoped she hadn't stolen from me, but this seemed like one of those problems where understanding would work better than a big stick. Although I wasn't very happy that my sixty bucks was missing.

I spent some fruitless time on the Internet and then looked through the property transfer documents and list of fires before deciding to give up on that to visit Carter directly. I didn't know what it was he was expecting me to confirm, but given the rate of fires in town and how I was a suspect, it was probably best not to waste any time.

At the *Harlot Bay Times*, I let myself in and discovered there was only Carter in the building, his arm still in a sling, packing boxes by himself. I didn't think it was possible, but he looked even worse than before. He certainly smelled like he hadn't been showering and had been possibly drinking at some point.

"We need to talk about the fires," I said to him.

Carter dropped a stapler into a box and then nodded for me to follow him to a small conference room. On the way I saw three offices with no staff. It appeared the *Harlot Bay Times* had ceased production. I didn't want to get into that at the moment since we had bigger problems to discuss.

"What did you get out of the papers I gave you?" Carter asked me, rubbing his stubble with his free hand.

"There have been a lot of property transfers, and sometimes the street names are misspelled and the numbers seem to change, and Coldwell and Gresso seem equally involved."

Carter sighed and rubbed his eyes.

"Did you bring the papers with you?" he asked.

I put them on the table. He shuffled through until he found the list of fires. He pointed to the one ten years ago where a woman had died.

"What can you tell me about that address?"

"There's a sporting complex there now, I think."

"That's right. Who bought the land and some of the

adjoining houses at least a year before this house burned down?"

I saw what he was getting at. Having studied the papers, I knew the answer immediately.

"Coldwell did."

"I really thought you were a better journalist than this," Carter said, his tone completely flat. I was in no mood to take any crap from him, but the truth was, he was probably right. I'd been reading through the property transfers and the list of fires and hadn't thought to connect them together to see who had bought land around the fires well ahead of time.

But I wasn't about to tell Carter that, so I ignored it.

"I don't think that's a smoking gun. Developers buy land all the time. Jonas Bishop, downstairs from my office, bought a couple of houses recently near that warehouse that burned out. Does that mean he's an arsonist?"

"I don't trust anyone not to be an arsonist now."

My phone rang. The name on the screen said *Kira*, which was strange since I was fairly sure I hadn't given her my phone number and certainly hadn't stored hers.

"Hello?"

"Harlow? It's me. Can you come down to the supermarket?"

"What's wrong?"

"I really need you to come down to the supermarket."

I had a sinking feeling in my stomach again.

"Okay, I'll be there in a minute," I said and hung up.

"I have to go now, then I'm investigating both Coldwell and Gresso."

"Gresso? He's got nothing to do with it. Don't waste your time. I want you to look at Coldwell."

"I get that he's evicting you, and he is a sleazy horrible person, but I am actually a good journalist and that means I'm going to do my research," I said.

I rushed out of there before Carter could answer me, jumped in my car and gambled that "the supermarket" was the closest one just off the main street.

When I arrived there, I saw the owner, Charles Vandenbosch, standing by the front door looking out into the street. When he saw me he quickly waved me inside. I followed him to his office, where Kira was sitting in a chair with her backpack in her lap, her feet huddled together, crouched down like she was trying to shrink herself out of existence. There was a block of cheese, some tampons, a bar of soap and a bottle of shampoo sitting on Charles's desk.

I knew what had happened immediately, but I had to sit through the excruciating explanation of how one of their staff members had observed Kira putting things in her backpack and then they'd stopped her. She'd screamed at them, then she'd opened her bag and they'd taken her to the back room and called me rather than the police. Throughout all this, Kira didn't say a word.

"Now, I understand this may have just been a mistake, a one-off thing. But she can't come back here for at least the next three months. If I or any of my staff see her in the next three months, we will call the police immediately. We have the video footage of her putting items in her bag and we will give it to the police," Charles said.

"I understand. I'm sorry about this," I told Charles. I stood up and motioned Kira to come with me.

She followed me out of the supermarket with her head down and we got into my car. I was going to drive back to my office but decided instead to take a long looping drive around Harlot Bay. I have read that talking to teenagers is easier on a car trip because you aren't looking directly at them and they don't have to look directly at you. My car coughed and grumbled but soon we were heading up into the hills above Harlot Bay and into the rich neighborhood. I glanced at Kira and noticed she was wearing a top that she definitely hadn't been wearing when she'd left my office. It was very new. Had she stolen it?

I was out of my depth.

We drove in silence, heading into the rich district, going up Barnes Boulevard, where Zero Bend had burned down part of his house during the Butter Carving Festival. There was scaffolding all around the house. It was probably eighty percent done being restored to its former state. Another few months and you wouldn't even know that there had been a fire.

As we drove I tried out various conversation openers in my head but then dismissed them all. I wanted to shout at her for stealing from a supermarket. I wanted to ask her what was wrong. I wanted to hug her. I wanted to tell her she could trust me and at the same time I wanted to throttle her.

Was this what it was like with teenagers? Although it pained me to admit it, perhaps I hadn't given the moms as much credit as I should have. After all, there had been more than one occasion when Molly, Luce or I had come home in the back of a police car.

We drove out of the hills and down into Harlot Bay in complete silence. By the time I returned to my office, I had decided on the only course of action that I could possibly make sense of. Despite my desire to throttle Kira, I pulled up outside my office and then just patted her on the hand before jumping out of the car. Kira followed, still scared, cowering like a dog that knows it's going to be beaten.

"So are you going to work at the bakery now? Do you want to go to the coffee shop or back with me? We have lunch at about twelve today," I said.

"Um... is going to the bakery okay?" Kira said, still as timid as a mouse.

"Okay, but you have to give me a high five first," I said. I put up my hand and Kira looked at it, clearly not understanding what was happening whatsoever. When I touched her on the shoulder she almost jumped out of her skin.

"The Torrent witches are not your family, which means we don't act like your family, okay? No one is going to find out about this unless you tell them."

Kira nodded, but didn't answer.

"See you later today," I said and then headed back upstairs into my office like nothing had happened.

CHAPTER SEVENTEEN

"So whose house are you staying at?" Molly asked.
"Sarah's," she replied.
"Is there anyone else who is staying there?" Luce asked, pointing a finger at Kira.
"No, just me and Sarah."
"What are you doing?" I asked.
"Watching some movies," Kira said. She saw me raise my eyebrows. "Watching some romantic comedy movies," she amended.
"Where are your secret party clothes?" Molly asked.
"Rolled up inside my spare clothes," said Kira.
"I think you're ready to lie your way into this party," Molly said.

Three days had passed with no more fires and no progress really on who or what might be causing them. I'd started doing a few more shifts at the bakery in an attempt to earn more money, and the only communication between me and Jack was phone messaging. I know we'd agreed to not see each other so Jack might have a chance of catching someone if they were following me, but that didn't mean I had to enjoy it.

True to my word, I'd kept Kira's shoplifting a secret, and thus far, it seemed the story hadn't spread.

After a day of walking around like a scalded cat, Kira finally relaxed. She must have realized no secret punishment was coming.

It seemed like she was finally starting to let her guard down. She trusted us enough to tell us that she wanted to go to a party being held at the house over on the edge of town.

Having long experience of the moms putting the kibosh on any party plans, we immediately got to work training Kira how to craft an effective lie so she could go out.

Hey, we weren't her mother! Besides, school holidays were coming to a close shortly, and soon she'd be back in school. The girl deserved to have a little fun.

"You think I'm ready? Really?" Kira asked.

"Ready as you'll ever be. Remember, short answers, don't seem too eager but don't seem too bored. You're asking permission, but it's not a big deal," Luce said.

"Okay, here I go," Kira said. She put her phone in her pocket and headed out the front door down to the main house. The moment she was gone, Molly turned to me, her face serious.

"I think Kira took some money from my bag," she said.

Oh no, I really *did not* want to have this conversation.

"And some more of my clothing has gone missing," Luce added. "You don't think she took it, do you?"

"I... don't know. I can't really say," I stammered.

"I asked Mom for more of the story about Kira and she told me she'd been shoplifting and stealing and skipping school. Now money is gone, we're missing clothing, and I don't think it was Adams taking the food from the fridge," Molly said.

"Is she in trouble of some kind? Is she planning to run away?" Luce asked.

They weren't asking like they wanted to get Kira in trouble and planned to slam her as soon as she walked back in the door. They were genuinely concerned why a teenager would steal money or clothing or food.

"Look, she might have, but I don't want to talk to her about it and I don't want to make a big deal. She has serious trust issues and if we pummel her over little things like this, we're not going to get anywhere," I said.

"But stealing? Are we supposed to overlook stealing?" Molly asked.

"You stole. You got away with it. And I'm sure the moms knew."

"I took one thing *one* time and then I felt so bad that I took it back. Was hardly stealing at all. More like *borrowing* for a couple of hours," Molly said.

"I don't think we should overlook stealing, but let's wait a bit longer. We need to take a gentle approach because we really don't know what's going on with her," I said.

Molly and Luce agreed with me that all three of us were very much out of our depth. I guess if we had children of our own we would have had years of dealing with big and small problems and might actually be able to come up with a response that worked. I had no doubt that Kira had taken money from Molly's bag and Luce's missing clothing as well. But I didn't really know what I could do about it. Search her room? Prove that she was a thief? Make her hate me so much that she wouldn't say another word?

"Do you remember that time we snuck out to the party on Truer Island?" Luce asked, changing the topic.

"Which one? The one where the rope broke on the tree swing? Or the one where you kissed Scott and then he sneezed and head-butted you?" Molly asked.

"Like your teenage romantic adventures were so good. What was the name of the guy you vomited on?" Luce said.

"Jeff something," I said.

"He still went out with me again," Molly said.

"I was talking about the time we went out to the party and had a huge bonfire and that crazy guy threw a firework in and we thought it was gonna kill everybody but it just shot up into the sky. It was *so* awesome," Luce said.

"Yeah, I guess it was pretty good," I said.

At the time, it seemed sneaking out to a party for illicit teenage activities was the most exciting thing in the world. On the other hand, some of those parties were boring and I can remember being cold and wishing I could go home, but sometimes I couldn't because I'd told some elaborate lie. One time the three of us ended up sleeping on the floor of my friend Peta's house and then had to get out of there at six in the morning before her parents woke up. That definitely wasn't fun.

We were talking about other parties and teenage misadventures when Kira came back in through the front door, her cheeks pink and grinning at us.

"It worked!" she said. We all cheered and hugged. Yes, we had orchestrated a lie and then she'd told it to the moms, but it wasn't a *big* lie.

"Okay, I'll take you," Molly said, jingling her keys.

CHAPTER EIGHTEEN

Today in the bakery there was an undernote of spice along with the cinnamon and sugar and the scent of delicious crusty bread. The moms were always adding something new to the menu and this week it was a spiced fruit bun. They wouldn't tell me what the spice was, but it had a warmth to it. When you bit into the bun, you got an initial burst of heat and then the back of your throat warmed. They were selling like crazy despite the fact that it was still summer and quite hot. The tourists couldn't get enough of them.

We were heading past the end of the lunch rush and I was handing over what I think was possibly my hundredth bag of spiced fruit buns. The air conditioner was doing its best to keep Big Pie at a reasonable temperature, but there were so many tourists flowing in and out that it was struggling.

Despite the heat, I was enjoying working at the bakery. One of the good things about working the rush is that you're too busy to think about anything much at all, which was a good thing since I was possibly facing a future of working at the bakery for many years to come.

Yesterday I'd attended a council meeting where Sylvester Coldwell had put forward his proposal to eliminate the free rent program. Dominic Gresso was there as well and spoke in support of it. Carter had managed to round up a few of the business owners to come to the council meeting to protest against it, but being that it was summer and peak tourist season, most of the owners hadn't been able to attend. The council had advised that they would take written submissions on the matter and then they'd hold a vote.

I handed another bag of spiced fruit buns over the counter, my mind slipping into the what-ifs of the free rent program being shut down.

First up, it would mean no more office space, which meant I would have to start working from home. That hadn't been so good in the past. There were just too many distractions, from a hungry cat who would keep asking for cheese to a comfy sofa to a bed, the fridge and everything else. It was also really easy to lose the structure of the day if you didn't have to go somewhere to work. Getting up a few minutes later one day led to a few minutes later the next day, and soon it was ten in the morning before you even opened your eyes. It wasn't just me who would be affected, either. There were a few businesses who didn't have any option to work from home, including a crystal shop that had opened only a month ago called Chaos Crystals. The owner, Shirley, used to work out of a rickety old bus she drove around. Now, she'd finally moved into an actual shop and it looked like Coldwell might be successful in shutting her down.

"I can't stop eating these spice buns," a woman said to me as I passed a bag to her over the counter.

"I know, they're delicious," I replied, returning to the here and now.

The line of tourists finally grew shorter, and eventually I got to the final customer, a sandy-haired man in his forties.

"Hi, what can I get you?" I asked.

"Sorry, I'm not here to buy anything. I was wondering whether I can place this flyer up in your front window. My daughter has gone missing and I'm looking for her," the man said.

I took the flyer he handed me. The missing girl was Sophira Barnes, sixteen years old. There were two photos of her, a reward offered and a phone number to call Wes Barnes.

My witch intuition had been dormant for quite a while now, but the moment I looked at the flyer, goose bumps ran down my arms and I shivered. I had the very strong feeling that Sophira was definitely somewhere in Harlot Bay.

"I'll put it up in the window. Do you have some I can leave on the counter?" I asked.

Wes gave me a handful of flyers.

"Thank you so much. She ran away a couple of months ago, and we used to live in Harlot Bay so I'm hoping she came here."

"Have you tried to talk to any of her friends?"

"They don't know where she is. Once school starts up again, I'll see if I can get the principal to put up some flyers."

"How long ago did you move out of Harlot Bay?"

"Four years ago. Just me and my daughter. Her mom passed away about six years before that. I know it's a long shot, but I don't know really where else to go."

"I'm sure you'll find her," I said. I know it was a clichéthing to say, but I was certain that he would find his daughter.

I couldn't tell him, of course, that I was a witch and my intuition was telling me he would find her, so I smiled and he went off to the next shop. I stuffed one of the flyers in my apron before another flood of tourists clamoring for spiced buns hit Big Pie.

CHAPTER NINETEEN

The blood drained from Kira's face the moment she saw the flyer.

When I'd come home from the bakery, I'd dropped it on the kitchen table (our go-to collection spot for every random piece of paper and junk mail that we received). I was sitting on the sofa with Adams in my lap, feeling my feet relax and working myself up to standing again so I could have a shower, when Kira arrived home with my cousins. They all looked worn out and smelled strongly of coffee. Despite this, they were all talking about the beach trip we had planned for tomorrow. Traveler would be closed for the big renovation Molly and Luce were sinking all their money into, and so we were all going to the beach for swimming, a barbecue and fun.

Molly and Luce were talking so much that they didn't see what I did. Kira stopped by the side of the kitchen table, and I saw the blood leave her face when she saw the flyer. She froze for a moment and then slowly reached out to touch the piece of paper as though it might strike at her with sharpened fangs. She looked at me, a quick glance, but it was full of guilt and not just that, but fear too. She then rushed off into her bedroom.

Molly and Luce were too wrapped in up in what they were talking about to notice, and I'm sure to them it appeared I was simply sitting with my feet up with Adams purring in my lap, but in my mind, giant puzzle pieces were thudding into place.

Aunt Cass had said there was a witch in town who was starting fires. By Kira's reaction to the flyer, I was sure that she knew Sophira Barnes. Not only that, I was sure that Kira was helping her by stealing food, clothing and money.

While my cousins talked their way through making a quick dinner, I sat on the sofa and tested my hypothesis from different angles. Yes, there was a giant leap of logic in there that just because Kira was a witch, Sophira was too, but something felt right about it. When Aunt Cass's cottage full of fireworks had caught fire and exploded, there had been a sweet scent on the spot, a hint of the magic that had caused the fire. I would have bet a thousand dollars that the missing girl, Kira's friend, was a witch, and when she started a fire that sweet scent would be there.

"Hello? Harlow? Ms. Torrent?" Molly said.

"What? Sorry, just thinking about something."

"Wow, thinking. Fancy. What's *that* like?" Molly teased.

"Is it a hobby or something you're planning on doing professionally?" Luce added, piling on.

I did the very adult thing and answered with that noise that goes *neena neena neena*.

"Did you want any of this satay chicken? Is Kira going to have some?" Molly asked.

I breathed in the scent of sweet peanut curry. Yes, it had come out of the jar, and if the moms found out we weren't "making meals from scratch" they'd probably get simultaneous headaches, but for a quick meal on a weeknight it was delicious.

"Serve it up," I said.

Luce called out to Kira, who eventually emerged from the bedroom and sat with us at the dinner table. I put the flyer away and focused my attention on talking to Molly and Luce and Kira like it was a standard night. Kira was back doing her nervous pet thing again, but after a while she relaxed and even started laughing when Luce teased her about how many cute hot boys in shorts would be at the beach tomorrow.

"And that includes *our* very cute hot boys, who will also be wearing shorts," Luce said.

I ate my meal and joked along with them. I had messaged Jack this morning and he had told me he hadn't come up with anything yet regarding the arsonist. He wanted to see me and I wanted to see him too, so I'd invited him to the beach tomorrow. Our plan to stay apart so Jack might have a chance to catch anyone who might be following me had gone nowhere, so we'd decided to abandon it.

I was too tired from a long day of work to think of a good plan regarding Kira and the missing Sophira Barnes. The best I had so far was to tail Kira. I was sure one day soon she would leave my office to work at the bakery and hoped no one would notice that the five-minute walk had taken her an hour.

Although my intuition was telling me that the missing girl was Kira's friend, part of me was very much hoping that she wasn't behind the fires. The empty houses and businesses that had burnt down weren't good, but at least no one had died.

But what if she'd started the fire that had killed Lenora Gray?

I knew the guilt of starting a fire you couldn't control very well. An entire apartment complex had burnt down because I had a bad dream, essentially. Then, a few days after I'd returned home, it had happened again.

We finished dinner and Kira took herself to bed early, tapping away on her phone.

For a moment, I admit that, yes, I considered breaking her privacy and sneaking a peek at that phone. There was definitely something there about "the greater good." Eventually I convinced myself that I shouldn't. It wasn't *entirely* pure ethical problems that stopped me, either. The fact was that Kira was attached to her phone like there was an umbilical cord. Short of sneaking into her room when she was asleep, there was simply no way I'd be able to get a look at it.

Once everyone had gone to bed, I crept back out to the main room and cast a very simple "wake me up" spell. I drew a line across the floor near the door with my finger. What the spell does is right there in the name: if anyone crossed the line, it would wake me up. If Kira went sneaking out, I'd be right behind her.

With that in place, I went to bed, and despite the thoughts of Kira initially dominating my mind, as I drifted off all I could think of was Jack, the golden sand and the beautiful calm ocean.

CHAPTER TWENTY

"I say we follow her. We'll get a crystal and do that tracking thing Kira suggested," Molly said.

We were on the beach with all the tourists, covering up with sunscreen and discussing our plan to find out the identity of Aunt Ro's secret mystery man.

"We need to test the tracking thing first, though, make sure it works," Luce said, rubbing down her arms.

"It definitely works. I've done it before. The problem is that the crystals to do it cost at least a hundred dollars and they're one use only. So unless you have a hundred for a test and then another hundred for real, you might have to trust that it's going to work," Kira said.

"We don't have two hundred right now," Luce said.

"So when you said that you are sinking every dollar you have into the renovation, you meant *literally* every dollar?" I asked.

"I think I have forty bucks left in my bank account," Molly said.

"You might have to buy the ice cream today," Luce added.

On the way to the beach we'd stopped at Traveler and had

a quick look inside before going on our way. The builders had been at work since daybreak and were planning to work late into the night to complete the transformation of Traveler from tourist shop that sold T-shirts and stickers to modern, comfortable, beautiful coffee shop that sold incredible coffee.

The coffee machine, or "Stefano" as Luce called it, was safely packed away in a back room so it couldn't be damaged. There were a veritable horde of men inside Traveler, demolishing, rebuilding and repainting. Molly and Luce were both so excited they could barely contain themselves. They hoped they would be able to reopen tomorrow, but the builders had warned they might need another day to let all the new paint dry.

"I have a few bucks," I said. "Maybe enough for chocolate ice cream."

"Ah do love me some chocolate," Luce said in her best Southern, starting with the sunscreen on her legs.

It was ten in the morning and the beach was full of tourists as far as the eye could see. We were quickly heading to the end of the holidays and this was the last big burst before Harlot Bay would finally start to settle down. There'd still be a lot of tourists through fall, and we even had people come in winter, but there was always this giant peak where it felt like everyone in the country had come to town.

Due to Truer Island and the curve of the bay, there were virtually no waves in the ocean. The water was gently lapping and creeping up the beach as the tide came in.

The boys hadn't arrived yet, so we eventually finished covering ourselves in sunscreen and headed out to the ocean. We were swimming around with all the tourists, laughing and splashing each other, when Luce spotted the boys on the beach and waved to them.

Will, Ollie and Jack had arrived together. Since being

hauled into the same family dinner some months ago that had eventually led to Will and Ollie becoming Luce and Molly's boyfriends, the two of them had become good friends, although really they couldn't be much more different. Ollie was a librarian who wrote a historical website about Harlot Bay and I think loved reading more than almost anything else in the world. Will worked with his hands all day building gardens. Yet the two of them had become the best of pals, and I think even Molly and Luce had been surprised when they'd discovered that Will and Ollie had gone out a few times just the two of them.

Now it looked like Jack was getting included in that circle as well. The three of them stripped off their T-shirts and came wading out into the ocean.

It was Kira who gave word to my thoughts.

"Oh my Goddess," she whispered, looking at the three very manly men walking out towards us. Will was a landscape gardener who hauled around bags of potting mix and plants and lumber all day, so he was a strong boy, and despite the fact that Ollie worked in the library, he looked like a rock star who on his days off hit the gym.

As for Jack... well, he'd been working renovating houses and was a former cop. He looked like someone had carved him out of rock. The three of them waded out where we were, Molly and Luce diving upon their boyfriends so fast they took both of them under the water.

I was too stunned to do anything like that. So I stood there with my mouth open, Kira the same beside me until Jack swam up, grinning.

"Hey, Harlow," he said.

I mumbled something, possibly about biceps, who knows, and sort of shook my head like I was waking myself from a concussion. Kira recovered as well, sinking up to her neck and swimming away a little, pulling her sunglasses down so she could observe from a distance. I finally found my voice.

"Hey, Jack," I said.

Jack dived under the water and came to the surface right in front of me, water pouring off him like he was a sea god. He kissed me quickly on the lips, tasting of salt. I laughed and tried to push him away from me, but it was like pushing a mountain.

I splashed him instead.

We spent the day swimming and relaxing on the beach. In the afternoon we snagged one of the free barbecues and let the three boys have at it, cooking up burgers and fried onion while we sat at a picnic table and opened a bottle of wine.

We had burgers and ice cream, and then around four in the afternoon we eventually said our goodbyes, tired but happy.

Luce and Molly gave their boyfriends very passionate kisses. Jack and I settled for a very demure kiss and a promise to meet up in a day or two for another lunch date.

We took a quick detour past Traveler, which had transformed since the morning. The new counter was in place, as were the tables and chairs. The builders were still working furiously, sawing and hammering seemingly everything in the shop.

We arrived home to find Aunt Cass waiting for us. She was sitting on the sofa stroking Adams like she was a Bond villain.

"Can I trust the two of you to keep a secret?" she asked, pointing a finger at Molly and Luce.

"Of course you can," Molly said automatically.

"We're like bank vaults," Luce said.

Aunt Cass scoffed at this, then must've decided she didn't want to get up off the sofa just so she could speak to me and Kira alone.

"I finished the new beacons and have them set up around town. The next time there's a fire, we'll get a precise location," she said.

"That's great," I said, looking at Kira out of the corner of my eye.

"Yeah, it's good," Kira mumbled.

Now that Aunt Cass had the new beacons up around Harlot Bay, it would only be a matter of time before we found the hidden witch. I still wasn't one hundred percent sure that it would be Kira's friend, but the slight flash a panic on her face strongly suggested it was.

"Why is that some big secret?" Luce asked.

"Your mother has very specific 'views' about me climbing up in high places."

"Like when you climbed to the top of the church spire because you were sure there was hidden treasure up there?" Molly asked.

"There *was* hidden treasure up there. Hidden historical treasure," Aunt Cass replied.

It was a few years ago now that Aunt Cass had climbed the peak of the highest spire of the tallest church. She'd pulled off the capstone to discover the stonemasons who'd built it had left some letters up there, along with a few coins, and one of them had left an entire journal. The historians of the town were very excited about this discovery and called it treasure, but it definitely wasn't the type of treasure that Aunt Cass had been looking for. She'd been searching for the *gold coin* type of treasure.

"Will we be able to find the hidden witch even if she doesn't start a fire?" I asked.

Aunt Cass shook her head.

"No, that's all I had to work with, so that's what it's tuned to. Unfortunately, we have to wait for something else to burn down."

"What do you mean *hidden witch?*" Luce asked.

"I'll let Miss-passionately-kisses-her-boyfriend and Miss-sneaks-out-to-a-party explain," Aunt Cass said, pointing at me and then Kira.

"How do you know I went to a party?" Kira said.

"You can't fool the cool. And I'm the cool," Aunt Cass said. She shooed Adams off her lap and went back to the main house.

"Dude, rookie mistake. Deny, deny, deny. Even if they have photographs of you doing it, you deny. She probably didn't know you snuck out to a party, she's only guessing. Then you confirmed it," Luce said.

"Oh, I didn't realize," Kira said, shrugging.

We were all sandy and tired from the day. After having showers, it was fend for yourself regarding dinner. None of us had the energy to go down to the main house, even though we knew there would be a spectacular meal. I end up eating a bowl of cereal, having a cup of coffee and then sharing a piece of cheese with Adams. He wasn't smelling like lavender anymore. I assumed this was either because he'd stopped visiting or perhaps because he was washing himself more thoroughly before he came home. I had once seen him swimming in a pond up around the back of the property trying to catch fish, so maybe he was dunking himself there.

It had been an amazing day. Molly and Luce were practically bouncing off the walls with happiness and excitement that the renovations at Traveler were nearly done. I was feeling happier than I'd been in a very long time. Yes, there had been good times since I'd moved back to Harlot Bay, and, no, this isn't that cliché thing where everything in your life is suddenly better because you meet a man.

There was something definitely there between us. Jack was staying in town, and despite the fact my online newspaper might fail and I'd have to spend a very long time working behind the counter of the bakery, I was feeling very happy about it.

I went to sleep with Adams at the foot of my bed, my dreams filled once more with the golden beach, lapping waves and a gorgeous man with eyes that verged on blue and green emerging from the sea in front of me.

CHAPTER TWENTY-ONE

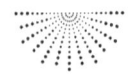

I woke up in pitch darkness with Adams's paw in my mouth.

"Get up! There's a fire at the bakery!" he yelled. He jumped off me as I fumbled my way out of bed so groggy I lost my balance and crashed into the wall. I hit the lights and nearly blinded myself. In a daze, I managed to get dressed.

"What do you mean?" I asked. Clearly the dumbest question in the history of time.

"You have to go to that bakery right now!" Adams yelled and ran off to wake the others. I rushed outside and started my car. The adrenaline had woken me up like a bucket of cold water to the face. I didn't bother waiting for Molly and Luce. I raced down the hill, seeing lights behind me as my family followed. I blew through a stop sign without obeying it and had to take a moment to force myself to slow down and take a deep, shuddering breath. It felt like I wasn't breathing at all, and then suddenly I was gulping air, as though I'd been suffocating. As I came into town I heard the howl of the fire siren. My hands were shaking so badly I could barely turn the corner.

Sheriff Hardy was already on site and his men had blocked the street. It was two in the morning, yet there were still a few tourists around and others coming out of their hotels. I pulled up in the street, not bothering to park my car properly, and promptly fell out on the road as my legs gave way. I got up, feeling my hands stinging, and stumbled down the street towards the roaring blaze that engulfed the Big Pie Bakery. Sheriff Hardy came towards me with his hands out and grabbed me in an enormous hug.

"No," I moaned, pain spiking into the very heart of me.

"I'm sorry, I'm sorry, they're trying to put it out," Sheriff Hardy said. He let me go as the rest of my family arrived. The moms rushed over, quickly followed by my cousins, Kira and Aunt Cass. Kira was as white as a sheet, shocked at what she was seeing. Aunt Cass was angry, baring her teeth at the fire as though she wanted to scare it into submission. Mom and Aunt Freya clung to each other, their faces anguished as they watch their life's work burn. Aunt Ro stumbled into Sheriff Hardy's arms. She sobbed as though her heart was breaking, and I suppose it was. They clung to each other, and through the terror and fear I saw it wasn't merely the sheriff and someone he had known for a long time. Sheriff Hardy kissed her on the cheek and was whispering frantically in her ear as she held on to his shirt, her tears leaving a wet patch on the front of it.

Aunt Cass looked around, counting the number of tourists, firefighters and police officers. Mom touched her on the arm and shook her head.

"There's too many," Mom said.

"I can do it," Aunt Cass replied, raising up her hand.

"No, it's too late," Mom said. She didn't grab Aunt Cass's arm but rather hugged her instead.

It seemed like time sped up. One moment Big Pie was fully ablaze, the fire raging red, and the next it was dark, the flames extinguished, the firefighters pouring gallons of water into our destroyed bakery. One of the firefighters gave a shout for everyone to get back, but there was no time for any of us to move. There was an enormous crack and then a crashing louder than I'd ever heard as the entire building collapsed in on itself. The firefighters kept pouring water on the rubble, dousing it to ensure there was no chance the fire could spread to the adjoining shops.

The entire family was watching in stunned silence when colored glowing lines appeared around us. The moms started in shock as they appeared. There was a deep red line leading up to the bakery and inside, terminating at I guess the point where the kitchen used to be. There was another red line leading off down the street.

"Is this you?" Aunt Freya whispered to me.

Kira, who had been sitting on the gutter nearby, started crying into her hands. But before I could comfort her, she stood up and ran away down the street. As soon as she was gone, so were the lines.

"I'm going after her," I told my family and didn't wait for a response. I took off down the street after Kira, following her around a corner. I heard footsteps behind me and glanced back to see Molly and Luce following. They'd both been crying just as I had, but I could see they were equally determined to find out who had done this and to exact vengeance upon them.

Kira was young and she was fast, but she had nothing on three witches burning with furious anger. Or perhaps she *wanted* us to catch up to her. In any case, it wasn't long before Kira stopped and we surrounded her. She was babbling.

"I'm sorry, I didn't mean to do it, I'm sorry," she said.

"Shh, it's okay. That wasn't you," I said, wrapping my arms around her.

"There was no magic there," Luce said, pointing back in the direction of the bakery.

The glowing lines appeared around us again. The deep red line that felt like fire stretched away from Kira and me, heading down the street before turning a corner.

"We need to find where that line goes," Molly said. She rushed off and returned a few minutes later with her car. We piled in and then followed the deep red line down the street.

"Is this a good idea? What if the person doing this sees us?" Kira said. I could see she was scared, terrified even, but there was no way the three of us would let this go.

"We're with you. We're going to stay together. You're safe with us," I told her.

Kira nodded and then cleared her throat.

"I know I am," she said softly.

The red line took a looping course through the streets before it finally left the center of Harlot Bay and went up into the rich district that overlooked the town. It finally turned into a driveway of an enormous mansion set far back on the block. It had a white gravel drive leading up to ornate front doors. The red line went through those doors.

We slowed as we drove past the property. There were lights up outside, illuminating the grounds. The house itself was dark except for a single light glowing around the edges of the curtain on the ground floor.

"What do you say? Do we go in?" Molly asked. We drove past the mansion and parked around the corner.

"For all we know, this place is just the next house the arsonist was to burn down. If we break in there we could get caught. Then Sheriff Hardy has to come to arrest us," Luce said.

"Or this is where the arsonist lives," I said, looking out the window at the side of the mansion.

"I don't want to go in there," Kira said.

Molly was chewing on her bottom lip and clenching her hands on the steering wheel. She was riding that thin edge between despair and fury where all of us were right now. But it was Kira's voice that finally got through to her. She wasn't about to make a scared teenage girl break into a mansion in the middle of the night.

"We'll come back in the day, figure out who lives here, put this place under surveillance," Molly declared.

By the time we drove back past the front of the mansion, the light on the bottom floor was out. We drove back down through the blackness of the hills and into Harlot Bay, returning to where Big Pie used to stand.

All the while my heart was aching like a sore tooth. Was this what it felt like to be broken? Would I even know? The night was dark, the streets lit only by the streetlamps, but it felt like all the pain of the world was crushing in on us. The moms had built Big Pie from the ground up and now it was gone.

CHAPTER TWENTY-TWO

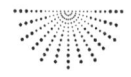

"Are we breaking the law being here?" I asked.

Jack continued to peer at the front window of the mansion through the binoculars.

"We're absolutely breaking the law being here," he replied.

It was the day after one of the worst nights of my life. Jack had come up to Torrent Mansion in the morning. Despite the horrors of last night, the moms had made breakfast for the guests and were generally putting on a brave face. Aunt Cass had retreated to her underground room and locked the door to the bottom part of the house with a spell so strong none of us could open it.

Jack had arrived early. Molly, Luce and Kira were still sleeping. Once we'd returned to Big Pie last night, we'd realized there was nothing we could do, so we'd come home. I'd spent the night tossing and turning, the anxiety only draining away late in the morning. It felt like I'd had maybe three hours sleep.

Jack brought me a file on Sylvester Coldwell that he'd acquired from some of his police friends. It seemed there had been an investigation around Coldwell using aggressive tactics to force people out of buildings that he wanted to buy. The police had stopped short of filing charges when one of the victims had recanted their story and then left town, refusing to participate further in the investigation.

"I think this is our guy," Jack said to me.

I hadn't been able to tell him, of course, about the red line that had led to the mansion, but I didn't have to. The police had Sylvester Coldwell under surveillance and they had seen him visiting the mansion.

So that's how we'd ended up in an empty vacation house directly across from the mansion, up on the third story, looking out an enormous glass window. Jack had used lock picks to get us in and we'd spent our time watching the place, waiting to see who might enter or leave. It was surprising it was vacant, given it was peak tourist season. My best guess was they wanted too much money for it.

We'd only been there a couple hours, but we'd been taking shifts at the window. I have to say it certainly wasn't the most romantic way to spend time with someone you liked.

I felt bad that I wasn't at home to help my family, but there wasn't really anything more I could do. Big Pie Bakery was utterly destroyed. The city had sent a bulldozer in the morning to push the rubble back so they could block it off and keep passing tourists safe.

If we were going to rebuild, it would take a long time. We hadn't talked about it at all, but I knew our family simply didn't have the money. The moms had borrowed against the bakery to help renovate the mansion last year after we'd been forced to move back into it, and then I think they'd borrowed against it again to help transform Torrent Mansion into a bed-and-breakfast. Now all they had was a block of land piled high with burned wreckage with a huge debt attached to it.

"Can you take a turn? I need to visit the bathroom," Jack said.

I took the binoculars from him and took his place at the window while he walked downstairs. It was all I could do to stop from crying at any random moment. I'd virtually grown up in the bakery, working behind the counter when I was six years old, standing on a stool and handing donuts over. That was before my dad left. It had been a fixed point for our entire lives and now it was gone.

My phone rang. Some unknown number, but I answered it anyway. It was Carter.

"I heard about the bakery. I'm sorry."

"Thanks."

"Did you find anything else on Coldwell?"

"Not yet. We're watching a house he visits sometimes, though."

Carter gave a long, drawn-out sigh over the phone.

"Last night, when someone set fire to the bakery, it seems that someone else took the opportunity to break into the *Harlot Bay Times*. They took three laptop computers with them. One of them contained all the research that I had gathered. I think it was Coldwell."

I pinched my nose between my fingers and tried to push back the tiredness that was throbbing in the back of my skull.

"Why do you think it was him?"

"I told him I wasn't going to be leaving, and he threatened me. Said he'd quote 'sort me out' unquote."

"Sounds like something he'd do," I said. I didn't precisely know the legality of the report Jack had acquired from his friend so I kept it to myself. Given that Coldwell had previously threatened people to get them out of places he wanted, it seemed very likely he'd done that to Carter. Stealing laptops, though, was something different.

"I'm going to be leaving town for a little bit," Carter told me.

"Where are you going?"

"Down the coast. I'll stay with my sister until my arm is healed. The *Harlot Bay Times* is going to be shut down until I decide to return, if I ever do."

I got the sudden absurd idea that Carter was going to ask me to write for the *Harlot Bay Times* or take it over, but instead he sighed again, said he'd see me around and then hung up.

I resumed focusing on the mansion across the road. The only sign of life in there had been a light flicking on around ten in the morning. So far no one had come or gone.

Jack returned from downstairs, and I gave him the update on what Carter had told me. By the time I was finished, Jack was shaking his head in disbelief.

"So is Coldwell harassing him to get him out, or do you think he knows that Carter has been investigating him?"

"Could be either option or both. I suppose it could be coincidence that the laptop with the research on it was stolen, but given how everything has gone so far I think it must be deliberate."

We talked for a while, going around in circles, chewing over what we knew. Of course, Jack was operating with incomplete information. He had no idea that there was a witch hidden somewhere in town who was possibly starting fires. He also had no idea that Kira had some power that showed us a line to the arsonist's next target or where he/she/it lived.

Time dragged on, taking us into the afternoon before finally a black shiny car turned into the driveway and drove up to the front of the mansion. Sylvester Coldwell got out. He went to the front door, opened it and went inside.

"Do you think we should call the police?" I asked Jack.

"Not yet. There is someone else living there, and I want to see who it is. I'm going to keep watching this place until they come out, no matter how long it takes."

There was something very cute about his determination, but I had to remind myself that Jack was on the hook, too. Whoever had been targeting me had gotten him as well by burning down the house that he'd been renovating.

My phone buzzed in my pocket. It was a message from Aunt Cass, telling me she'd found a possible location on the hidden witch. She asked me to go there immediately and sent the address.

I told Jack I had to go, gave him a kiss on the cheek and then crept out of the empty house and away to where my car was parked three streets away. The address was just on the other side of Harlot Bay.

I drove down through the hills, alternating between chewing over all the evidence and just being completely blank in my mind. I was so tired, the exhaustion of the previous night catching up with me, and it felt like I'd been sad for so long that I was emotionally worn out too. It was getting to the point where I couldn't even feel sad anymore.

I was sitting at a stop sign, staring blankly at nothing, when that nothing resolved into Kira. She was coming out of the other main supermarket in town carrying a bulging plastic bag full of groceries. She scurried off down the street after loading the groceries into her backpack.

I abruptly decided the time for soft kid gloves was done. We had two suspects for the fires – one was a sleazy real estate developer, but the other was a witch hidden somewhere in town, and I was now absolutely sure Kira was helping her. Even if she was only starting *some* of the fires, she had to be stopped. I parked my car and hurried after Kira. The streets were packed with tourists, so it was easy to stay out of sight. My intuition was telling me I didn't need the address Aunt Cass had just sent me.

Kira didn't look behind herself once. She seemed very determined and focused as she rushed out of the main part of town. I risked a little magic to cast a concealment spell just in case she *did* look behind her. I was already tired, and the concealment spell certainly didn't help me stay awake.

I yawned as I followed Kira. We were about three streets from the center of town when she turned at a rusted gate and vanished.

Yup, it was the address Aunt Cass had sent.

I hurried up to the house and looked into the yard. It was unkempt and the house looked like it had been empty for quite a long time. Sadly, it is the tale of a dying seaside town. Owners try to sell their houses and fail, and then many simply move away in desperation.

There was an old for sale sign sitting against the fence. Sylvester Coldwell's greasy smile was flaking and sun-damaged. I went through the gate and up to the front of the house. At the door I let the concealment spell go. It was too tiring to keep it going, and right now I didn't care if Kira saw me or not. With that, I pushed open the door and marched into the house. I could smell smoke, as though someone had lit a fire recently.

Like the other abandoned house we'd been to, the previous owners had left their furniture behind. I followed the sound of voices, Kira's and another girl's. I found them in the living room. It looked like someone had been living there for months. There were food wrappers everywhere. Next to a pile of junk mail I saw ashes, still warm from being set alight. Aunt Cass must have detected that accidental fire.

The girl was digging into the bag of groceries, pulling open a loaf of bread like she hadn't eaten in days. I didn't need the flyer with me to know that she was Sophira Barnes. Kira turned around when I walked in.

"What are you doing here? Did you follow me?" Kira said.

I was tired and, yes, there was plenty of anger built up from yesterday and the fire at Big Pie, but it broke my heart when both girls looked at me with fear in their eyes.

"Who is she?" Sophira asked, her voice quavering.

"Her name is Harlow. I'm staying with her," Kira said. I took a step forward, but Sophira jumped back as though she was afraid I would grab her.

"Don't come any closer!" she yelled.

The magic around me pushed and pulled, like the wind before a storm hits.

"It's okay, I'm –"

"Did my dad send you?" Sophira said.

The magic called, and a pile of junk mail on the table burst into flame. The scent of sweet honey hit me.

Sophira *was* the hidden witch.

Kira whirled around to face her friend.

"She's a friend, she helped me!"

But there was no getting through to her. Sophira backed away from the pile of burning junk mail, her face a mask of horror.

"I can't stop it," she gasped.

I didn't have the energy for this, but I'd been training with Hattie Stern for a while now, and so I reached for the flame, grabbed it and pulled all of the heat directly out of it. The fire was extinguished immediately and then I was holding a burning ball of hot air. I took a deep breath and lifted it up into the air before slowly releasing the ball of heat. It expanded, and the temperature in the room shot up a few degrees as the ball disappeared.

Once that was done, I took a few more deep breaths and fought the feeling that I wanted to light a fire to do it again. I heard Kira talking to Sophira, but I couldn't really focus on what they were saying. For a brief few minutes they were simply warm-blooded mammals that I could pull the heat out of. It wasn't long before the crest of the wave of desire passed and I returned to reality, finding myself sweating and almost shaking with exhaustion. Kira was standing by the bag of food, watching me cautiously.

"That was amazing," she said when I looked up.

"Ta-da!" I said weakly.

I saw that they'd been making peanut butter sandwiches before I'd arrived, so I asked Sophira to make me one. She did and soon I was gulping it down, feeling like I hadn't eaten for weeks.

When I finished the sandwich, I was feeling better. The two girls were still looking at me like I might turn into a monster in any moment, though.

"Sophira, I don't know why you ran away. But you're starting fires, which is something I have experience with. Come with me to the mansion up on the hill and we'll look after you. We won't even tell your dad unless you want us to."

Sophira looked at Kira for assurance.

"You can trust her."

"But what's going to happen? I'm not going back home again. I need to be in Harlot Bay, or the magic escaping is much worse."

"I'll introduce you to my Aunt Cass. She'll help you get the fire under control. We can give you a proper bed to sleep in, and then we can figure out what to do," I said.

Sophira glanced across at the couch she'd obviously been sleeping on for quite some time. Had she been staying in this house since she'd arrived in Harlot Bay? She'd been relying on Kira to bring her food and clothes for quite some time.

The moment trembled like a soap bubble. I was too

exhausted to say anything, which actually was probably a good thing. Eventually, Sophira nodded her agreement.

We gathered up her things, including Luce's blue cardigan and some other clothes that I recognized as Molly's. I took those and stuffed them in a separate bag. I had enough on my plate without confirming that Kira *had* actually stolen these. I'd wash them and then put them back in my cousins' closets like they were never gone in the first place.

When we arrived at the mansion, Aunt Cass was sitting on the front porch waiting for us. She came over to the car and gave both Kira and Sophira an appraising look. Sophira couldn't stop looking at Aunt Cass's pink streak and the silver nose piercing.

"You three come with me. We're going to boil some water," Aunt Cass said.

We left everything in the car and followed Aunt Cass up around the back of the mansion and into the forest. This whole area has had generations of Torrents build things and then abandon them. We always need to be careful because there are a lot of empty wells around the place and some full ones, too.

I walked along beside Aunt Cass, Kira and Sophira whispering behind us. I heard Sophira ask if Aunt Cass was cool and Kira answer that she was.

I know Aunt Cass was pretending she wasn't listening, but I saw the tiniest curve of a smile on the edge of her mouth.

Soon we reached a giant well that was full to the top. It had waterlilies growing across the top of it, and I knew a family of frogs lived nearby.

Aunt Cass waved a hand at the pond and then made a lifting motion. The magic around us pulled, and suddenly all the frogs in the pond came to the surface and hopped away.

"Wow," Sophira said.

"Can you teach me that?" Kira asked.

"Of course I can teach you that. You only have to ask," Aunt Cass said and then winked at her.

Despite my very tired state, I felt a little touch of jealousy.

"Why didn't you ever offer to teach me that spell?" I asked, a tiny bit more petulant than I really intended.

Aunt Cass turned to look at me.

"All you need is the desire to be taught. That's how it has always worked."

In a better mood (with more sleep) I might have just brushed it off, but it stung more than it should have. I guess she was right. Our mothers and Aunt Cass were happy to teach us magic, but it was only if we asked. For an instant, I saw the view of myself through my mother and aunts' eyes, much the same way as I saw Kira. They loved me and wanted to help me but often didn't know what was going on inside my mind.

If I'd really wanted to learn more, they would have taught me, but the fact was... I hadn't wanted to learn. I really hadn't wanted to be a witch at all given my out-of-control Slip magic was ruining my life.

"Okay," I said, looking down at the ground.

Aunt Cass whacked me on the shoulder.

"Learn how to do this," she said.

Aunt Cass gave a quick demonstration of a spell used to heat up water. Even I hadn't learned this one. After a few practice tries, the three of us were ready to go.

I cast the spell and a tiny swirl of steam rose up from the well.

"Good job, Kira next," Aunt Cass said.

Kira cast the spell and did even better than me. Steam rose from the well. Then it was Sophira's turn.

"I haven't done any magic on purpose for a long time," she explained to Aunt Cass.

"Well, we're Torrent witches and we do magic all the time, so let's go," Aunt Cass said and pointed at the well. Sophira took a breath and cast the spell. I could feel the magic swirling around us.

Normally for a spell like this, there would be a little tug as the witch accessed some of it. In Sophira's case it was a mighty *heave* as years of pent-up magic was released into the well. Within a few seconds the well water was boiling.

We all had to step back to get away from the radiating heat.

"Keep going!" Aunt Cass yelled out.

The well was bubbling furiously, the steam billowing up into the air. Another minute more and the magic jerked again as the entire well boiled dry.

As soon as the well was empty, Sophira put her arms down and relaxed, sitting down on the grass very quickly.

"Oh my Goddess," she sighed and then lay on her back.

Aunt Cass came to stand over the top of her.

"You need to use your magic or it will break out at random times," she told her.

Sophira looked sleepily up at Aunt Cass.

"Thank you," she whispered. Then she was asleep right there on the grass in the warm sun.

CHAPTER TWENTY-THREE

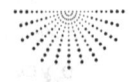

Two days and two nights passed by, the world feeling broken, but then slowly starting to move in its old rhythm. Aunt Cass explained to the moms that Sophira would be staying with us for a while. She told Kira her Slip Witch training was almost complete and soon she'd be able to get back to her family. Aunt Cass then arranged with Hattie for both of the girls to stay there.

It had taken a day for Sophira to finally agree to call her father, who came rushing up to the mansion.

There was a very tearful reunion out the front of the Torrent Mansion, and then Aunt Cass took him aside to talk. She told me later that night that his wife had been a witch who had died many years ago. Sophira and her father had stayed in town until four years ago, when he'd taken a job two states away. Growing into a teenager, Sophira hadn't used her magic since her mother died and it had started to lash out during inopportune moments. She'd been blamed for setting a fire in a chemistry lab at her school, and since then, anytime something went wrong she got the blame for it. Eventually she'd run away, coming back to Harlot Bay, where the swirling magical confluence helped calm her. Unfortunately it hadn't been enough, and when she was stressed, she started fires. She hadn't known she was starting the large fires, and Kira didn't know either.

Aunt Cass took me, Kira and Sophira down to her map which showed all of the fires across Harlot Bay. Sophira had started the fire in the stone cottage, destroying Aunt Cass's fireworks, and had started one of the other three fires that had occurred much earlier in the month. She had not caused any of the other fires. That was an intense relief for us and her but still left open the question of who precisely was responsible for Lenora Gray's death and all the other fires.

There was still a lot of unfinished business. Sophira's father was going to spend a few days in town, and then he'd return home to begin packing up their house so he could move back to Harlot Bay. In the meantime, Sophira and Kira would stay with us before eventually moving back with Hattie.

Jack was still at the empty vacation home across from the mansion, watching and waiting for someone to come out. I'd visited him every day, now adding food delivery to my list of jobs, but the only thing he reported happening was that Sylvester Coldwell had come and gone again and no one else had left the premises.

Sheriff Hardy came to the mansion and told us Detective Moreland was still in town but his investigation was no longer focused on us. What that meant, he wouldn't say.

The big romantic news was Sheriff Hardy openly kissing Aunt Ro in front of us, and despite how bad all of us felt, we hit him with some good-natured teasing. We hadn't gotten quite to the bottom of it yet, but the story as we understood it was Aunt Ro and the sheriff weren't together the night that we'd invited him to the family dinner (as a buffer, I might add). However, that *was* the night they'd started to get to know each other better, and then they'd started dating in secret. When we'd followed Aunt Ro to her so-called yoga class, she was in fact visiting Sheriff Hardy! He was the mystery man in the car Luce and Molly had seen a few days ago.

Aunt Freya and my mom were just as shocked as anybody that somehow this had been going on under their noses and were huffing and puffing about it, but then Aunt Ro made some pointed comments about one of the bank managers in town to Mom and one of the local farmers to Aunt Freya. Both of them had shut down *that* conversation with lightning speed before we could get any more information out of them.

As soon as we were all feeling better, we were definitely going to be digging into these new romantic developments.

So that was how two days went by. Two days since the bakery was destroyed, two days since the world cracked in half. Aunt Cass's improved beacons had finally worked – Sophira had accidentally set some junk mail alight shortly before I'd found her by following Kira.

The world was calm, but not for long.

CHAPTER TWENTY-FOUR

"Suuuure, you're going to a movie. Uh-huh, I know your game, I used to play it," I teased Kira as I drove her and Sophira to the movies.

"We are legit going to the movies. I promise. Cross my heart," Kira said, laughing.

"Does the cinema still have that back door that opens into the alleyway?"

"Of course it does!" Kira said.

"But we're not using it. Promise," Sophira added.

"Rookie mistakes all around. Too much promising and the mark gets suspicious," I said, waving my finger at Sophira in the mirror.

We turned a corner and then a sudden surge of magic hit the car. It was so strong it was lucky I didn't drive us into a building. All I could see for a moment was flame, roaring, filling my vision. I blinked and then there was a solid line of fire, stretching out from the three of us, down the road and around the corner. I managed to pull over, all of us gasping for a solid minute before we could calm ourselves.

There was another wave and the hot coal in my belly

reappeared. Fishhooks in every muscle began pulling at me, urging me to get closer to whatever was at the end of that line.

"That's the one who keeps burning things," Sophira said through gritted teeth.

"It hurts Harlow," Kira groaned, her hands over her stomach.

"We have to follow it," Sophira said.

I could barely think. The pain in my stomach was agony, and the pull in my muscles was like I hadn't drunk water for a week and now there was an inviting cool stream in front of me.

I started the car, and we drove somewhat mindlessly through the holiday traffic, following the throbbing line of fire up the hill. The closer we got, the better we felt.

I followed the line of fire up a long white gravel drive and leapt out of the car, Kira and Sophira close behind me.

Some distant part of me whispered that Jack would be watching from the house across the road, but I couldn't stop myself.

It was Sophira who kicked the door open, and then we all rushed inside. The mansion was old money. Polished wood floors, multiple stories, much like the Torrent Mansion but obviously it had never gone to ruin. Everywhere you looked there was more wealth. Expensive paintings on the walls, thick rugs, vases that had been broken and repaired with gold. But there were no flowers in those vases and the paintings were covered with a thin layer of dust. The place looked like it hadn't been cleaned in a long time.

There was a clear trail of footprints where Sylvester Coldwell had come and gone.

"Be careful," I told the girls as we followed the line. It went around the corner into a large open ballroom. There was an open fireplace on the far side, a roaring fire burning within.

The red line stopped there. It was stifling hot.

The room was mostly empty. A few pieces of furniture were scattered about the place. In a semicircle on the floor near the fireplace were photographs. It looked like someone had been wadding them up and throwing them into the fire. One had clearly charred before falling back out on the floor.

The three of us stood in front of the fire, staring at it for a moment before the pull receded, leaving us with our reason and thought and realizing we'd just rushed into a mansion following a magic line of fire.

"Let's get out of here," I urged.

It was too late. The doors we'd entered through were slammed shut by a man who must have been hiding behind them. He bolted them before turning around to face us.

It was Dominic Gresso. He wasn't dressed in his standard real estate garb but rather a stained black-and-white T-shirt and a pair of blue shorts that had clearly seen better days.

"What are you doing, Dominic?" I called out, looking around. There was only one other exit from this room and it had furniture piled in front of it.

He took a step towards us and I saw instantly that I'd been mistaken. This wasn't Dominic. A twin?

"No, no, no, you're wrong wrong wrong, do you like like like my fire?" the man said in a high-pitched singsong voice.

I stepped forward and pushed the girls behind me. The man didn't appear to have any weapons, and while I was scared, I was also a Slip Witch backed up by two other witches. If that guy came near us, he would get to see some fire very up close and personal. "What's your name?" I called out to him.

"Hendrick. Hendrick and Dominic. Dominic and Hendrick. Yes yes yes," he replied. He walked over to a side table to grab something. When he turned back to us, he had a long heavy fire poker made of black iron in his hand.

"Open the door. We want to leave," I told him.

"You have to see the fire fire fire," Hendrick said, lazily swinging the fire poker from one hand to the other.

"He's crazy," Kira whispered behind me.

"Don't worry, we'll get out of here," I told them. Hendrick was still moving closer, walking across the room, sometimes stepping through the glowing line of fire that only the three of us could see.

He was still between us and the door, and despite him being overweight like Dominic, I didn't want to risk running past him.

I was sweating, the stifling heat of the ballroom making my clothes stick to me.

"If I hit him with a fireball, I might pass out, so you'll have to drag me out with you," I whispered to the girls.

"Fireball fireball fireball," Hendrick repeated.

"Get away from us," I called out.

Our silent prayers for intervention were answered. Someone bashed on the door and called out.

My hope that it was Jack vanished when I heard the voice. Hendrick clapped his hands and ran back over to the door to unbolt it. In came his brother Dominic. Hendrick then bolted the door behind him. As soon as Dominic saw us, a look of panic crossed his face.

"What have you done?" he asked his brother, grabbing him by the arms.

"I want them to see the fire!" Hendrick said.

"Let us out of here, Dominic," I called out, my voice echoing across the large room. Dominic walked across to us, telling his brother to stay at the door. When he was halfway across the room, I yelled at him to stay there. He stopped in the middle of the room.

"You have to promise me you won't tell anyone," he pleaded.

"Tell anyone what? We just want to get out of here," I yelled back. Dominic turned around and called out to Hendrick to unlock the door, but he just laughed and started swinging the fire poker around in front of him.

"Hendrick, open the door or you'll never get to see a fire again," Dominic yelled.

"Fire, fire, fire," Hendrick repeated.

The red line in the middle of the floor had stayed in place through all this. But now it shook, a shimmer running through it before it split into three lines. One crept to encircle Dominic, surrounding him like an aura. The other surrounded his brother. The third line streaked across the floor to hit Sophira.

It spiraled up her body and plunged into her heart.

The magic heaved and the scent of honey filled the room.

"I know you," Sophira said, her voice cold. She pointed a finger at Dominic. "You're the one who bought our house after it burnt down!"

"I don't know, I don't remember," Dominic said. He turned around again to his brother.

"Open the door! Hendrick, it's too hot in here! They're going to leave now."

"And you're the one who started the fire!" Sophira yelled, pointing her finger at Hendrick.

A puzzle piece twisted into place. Fires, dates and names lined up.

"What's your last name?" I said to Sophira.

"I'm Sophira Laroche. Barnes is my dad's name. I started using it after my mom died in the fire he started!"

Abigail Laroche was on the list of fire victims. Sophira's mother and a witch. She'd died in the fire and was survived by her husband and daughter.

Witches are matriarchal. We don't take our husband's last name, but in this case Sophira had used her father's name after she had moved away from Harlot Bay.

In the moment it all came together I realized what was going to happen next, but I was powerless to stop it. There were scattered photos all over the floor, pictures of houses that Hendrick had burnt down or had planned to. I saw the bakery and me standing behind the counter.

My eyes tracked to a house painted blue with a white picket fence.

The sweet scent intensified and the photo burst into flames. Three more quickly followed before I could take another breath.

"No, it's not true," Dominic pleaded.

"*You* killed my mother and then *you* bought the ashes of our home!" Sophira said, pointing her finger at Dominic. Her voice sounded like that of an angry god from the sky about to strike down with all of the vengeance in the world. The temperature in the room spiked, making it almost too hot to breathe.

Dominic clearly didn't realize the danger he was in. For some reason he knelt and put his hands to the wooden floor before standing up again. Hendrick walked over to him with the fire poker in his hand.

"What did you do?" Dominic roared.

"Come to see the fire fire fire," Hendrick said with a sly little smile.

That was when the floor cracked open, an enormous hole appearing near the locked door, flames roaring up from underneath.

It wasn't a magical fire created by a distraught witch. The lunatic Hendrick must have set fire to the mansion before we'd arrived. We'd been pulled by his madness, somehow dragged by the connection between him and Sophira, and now we might die here.

Sophira screamed a note of pure rage and more of the photos burst into flames. To our right, the floor cracked open and a gout of flame lashed out, nearly touching the ceiling. This one definitely *was* magical. I could feel it pulling on the magic around us as Sophira's rage and fury took form.

Hendrick clapped and laughed, grabbing at his brother's arm and pointing at the new flames.

"Fun fun fun, see see see?"

There was another crack as the floor between us split, flames forming a wall and separating us from Dominic and his insane brother.

"Sophira, you have to stop, please. We need to get out of here," I yelled over the sound of the roaring flames.

"He destroyed my family," Sophira growled.

Just as I was about to punch Sophira in a desperate attempt to knock her out, Kira stepped in front of her and took hold of her hands.

"Remember what I was teaching you. You have to center yourself. Take a breath, relax. If we take them out of here with us, they'll go to prison forever," Kira said.

For a moment the magical flames roared higher as Kira battled with the desire to burn Dominic and his brother to death. She'd likely kill us too, unintentionally, her pain was so great.

But then she took a breath and the magical flames all subsided.

"Okay," Sophira said, pressing her forehead against Kira's.

The wall of flames between us and Dominic and his brother were not magical, unfortunately. I grabbed hold of the girls and skirted around them. The air was full of smoke, choking us, and the entire room was ablaze. All I could hear was the cracking sound of wood burning. If this mansion was like ours, it probably had complete floors beneath us. They were on fire and it wouldn't be long before the entire mansion collapsed. Hendrick ran towards us, trying to stop us from leaving, but Kira thrust out a hand and the fire poker flung across the room and embedded itself in the wall. Then she swiped a hand at the door and it smashed off its hinges.

The corridor was filled with flame, too intense for us to run through.

There was no escape.

"I've got this," Sophira yelled.

I sure as hell hoped she did, because I could barely breathe and couldn't see for the smoke and flames. The magic pulled around me and then we were standing in a clear spot, like a bubble, that was as cool as a fresh winter day.

Kira yelled out and suddenly Dominic and Hendrick were in front of us, running. We bolted after them, the bubble of cool and clean air making a passage for us. As soon as we passed, the flames roared in behind us. I could feel the soles of my shoes melting.

Before Dominic reached the front door, Jack smashed it open. He pulled Dominic and his brother out and then the three of us collided with him, crashing out of the mansion and landing on the gravel outside. We scrambled up and ran away from the mansion.

"They're the ones who burned the houses!" I yelled, pointing to Dominic and Hendrick. Dominic was trying to pull his brother away from the burning mansion but wasn't having much luck. Jack raced over to them and shoved both of them facedown onto the ground and told them to stay there if they ever wanted to walk again.

The scream of the fire engines made itself known over the roaring sound of the mansion going up in flames. Something exploded inside and the windows shattered outward, littering the ground with bits of broken glass and flaming embers. It wasn't long before the fire department was there and then the police. Dominic was pleading with his brother to shut up, but he kept talking about the fire and laughing, pointing, saying it was the best one yet. It wasn't long after that we were being treated for minor burns, and sometime later I found myself standing by the side of an ambulance with Jack in front of me, my hands around his waist, my head against his chest, listening to the slow beat of his heart.

CHAPTER TWENTY-FIVE

I was sitting in the park, sipping the last of my very delicious coffee supplied by the new and revamped Traveler. It's amazing how quickly things can change. Just a week ago I'd escaped a blazing mansion, and now here I was wearing some awesome 1950s-style swing clothing, waiting for my... I guess you could say boyfriend?... to return with ice creams to follow our spectacular lunch (Jack's famous sandwiches).

It was still summer, but a fall day must've come early because it was cooler than usual, which made it just perfect for sitting in the park and having a picnic.

Things had broken, but now they were well on their way to be repaired.

Big Pie Bakery was gone, burnt to the ground, but that hadn't stopped the moms. Not one bit. They had immediately started baking out of the home kitchen and were doing delivery runs around town with their baked goods. There was even a fundraiser planned to help rebuild the bakery coming up in a week once the latest wave of media buzz that had swamped the town faded away. The rash of fires in Harlot Bay hadn't made the mass media until the bakery had burned and everyone realized at once that there was actually an arsonist at work. As usual, all the major reporting networks descended on the town just so they could stand on the beach with the waves behind them and solemnly make statements like "this sleepy seaside town is once again the scene of tragedy..." with their fake faces on. Their desire to drag out the story to try to make it even bigger was squelched when Dominic's brother Hendrick readily confessed to setting the fire that had burnt down Big Pie. He'd been behind quite a few fires (including the one that killed Lenora Gray) and although Dominic claimed that he was mentally ill and insane, eventually he'd given in and confessed that he'd known about his brother's behavior. The story had turned very dark when it was discovered that Dominic had occasionally fed his brother addresses of properties that he wanted to buy. Hendrick would then try to burn them down. It appeared Big Pie Bakery was one of those addresses. Dominic wanted it burned down to put financial pressure on the moms so they would then sell Torrent Mansion. We discovered that Aunt Cass had pretended to be April and had called both Dominic and Coldwell to tell them she wasn't interested in selling. This had apparently prompted Dominic to set Hendrick loose.

The police were now digging into all of Dominic Gresso's real estate dealings and those of his father, who had died in the late 1980s. His cause of death was listed as a heart attack, but the story had come out that the family had paid off a local coroner to say that. In fact, Dominic and Hendrick's father had died of burns suffered to his body after a fire he'd set turned against him.

Dominic had even apparently handed over his father's journals, which contained information on other crimes committed in building their real estate empire. He was doing everything he could to reduce his eventual prison sentence.

As for Sylvester Coldwell, he was denying he knew anything about the arson. He claimed he and Dominic were old friends and he was merely visiting Hendrick, who rarely left the mansion. Thus far, Detective Moreland hadn't found anything, but we suspected it wouldn't be long before Coldwell went down.

Not everything was wrapped up nicely, but it was good enough for government work.

I took the last sip of my delicious coffee and let out a sigh as I looked across the park. The big peak of tourists had passed, and although the town was still packed, it would slowly drop away until it was ours again. Traveler was looking amazing, fully renovated, and now Molly and Luce were making money hand over fist. They were making so much that within six months they might be able to pay to have Big Pie rebuilt.

Kira and Sophira had moved to Hattie's house two days ago. I admit I already missed having the two teenagers around. Yes, they were snarky and sometimes sullen and would probably die if they didn't look at their phone every thirty seconds, but they were also hilarious and warm and, most of all, brave. In my brief conversation with Aunt Cass, she'd told me that Hattie had agreed to take it easier on them.

During my daydreaming, I suddenly felt a presence next to me. I looked up, hoping to see Jack carrying two ice creams, but it was John Smith instead, looking down at me. I quickly glanced around. There wasn't anyone nearby, so it was safe to talk.

"Hey, John," I said, giving him a smile.

"Talica Moore, I presume. You and that dress are looking fine," he said.

The smile froze to my face as I frantically tried to think of what to do. Obviously John had mistaken me for someone else. But this was amazing news! Talica Moore! Who was that? I had to be careful. He might reveal more that I could use to track down who he actually was.

"The one and only," I said and winked at him.

John smile grew broader and he winked back. Whoever he thought I was, he obviously liked her very much. Maybe his girlfriend? Wife? Then his grin faltered and he frowned at me. The air around us chilled as though a cloud had covered the sun.

"I'm cold and it's dark. I'm stuck. Why did she interfere?"

"Who interfered?"

John jumped back, scared, and when he next looked at me, I knew that he was no longer seeing whoever this Talica Moore was.

"Harlow," he said, his voice rough. I saw Jack over to my right, walking towards us, an ice cream in each hand. John looked across at him and then down at me.

"I see it's all on track, then. Time to do it again."

"Do what?" I asked.

"What? Sorry, did you ask me something?" John said.

"Here, quick, take it before it melts," Jack said, rushing up and handing me a dark chocolate ice cream in a waffle cone.

The feeling of cold vanished the moment John forgot everything. I smiled at Jack and took the ice cream. Jack sat down beside me, taking a bite of his peppermint chocolate chip.

John looked at the two of us and then waved happily, putting his hand over his mouth to indicate he knew I couldn't answer when someone else was around who wasn't a witch.

"See you later, Harlow! So good to see you found someone!" John said happily before fading away.

"Something wrong?" Jack asked. I turned to him and

looked into those beautiful eyes. Today they were more green than blue. In the sunlight they were almost emerald.

"Everything is okay. I think," I said.

I kissed him, tasting the faintest hint of peppermint on his lips from the ice cream, smelling the freshly cut grass around us and hearing the sound of the seagulls high above squawking against the wind.

"I really think everything is going to be okay," I repeated. I didn't know what had happened with John – something seemed to tug at my mind like a word lost on the tip of my tongue.

I looked at Jack. There was something deeply right about this former tourist sitting with me under the warm sun.

I just knew everything would be okay.

AUTHOR NOTE

Read Fabulous Witch (Torrent Witches #4) now!

Thanks for reading my book! More witch stories to come. If you'd like an email when a new book is released then you can sign up for my mailing list. I have a strict no spam policy and will only send an email when I have a new release.

I hope you enjoyed my work! If you have time, please write a review. They make all the difference to indie Authors.

In the next book Harlow faces off with a deadly saboteur intent on killing a movie star.

xx Tess

TessLake.com

CPSIA information can be obtained
at www.ICGtesting.com
Printed in the USA
LVHW100718260322
714477LV00020B/287

9 781547 178766